The Angel Tree

The Angel Tree

DAPHNE BENEDIS-GRAB

Scholastic Press / New York

Library of Congress Control Number: 2014005098

ISBN 978-0-545-61378-1

10 9 8 7 6 5 4 3 2 1   14 15 16 17 18

Printed in the U.S.A.   23
First edition, October 2014

The text type was set in Horley Old Style MT.
Book design by Abby Kuperstock

For my sister, Sam

The Angel Tree

Prologue

It happened every year, late at night, long after darkness had settled over the small town of Pine River. No one knew who it was that got up in the icy midnight hours to erect the towering evergreen, its branches thick and full. But each year it would appear in the town square, the green pine and the strings of glowing lights a lone splash of color against the slate gray of the Town Hall and the powdery snow. The first person to see the tree was always Harold Dobbs, the village trash collector, who began his day before the rays of the frosty sunrise spread across the blanket of snow covering the town. The sight of the tree would warm him against the biting cold of the Pine River winter and he would linger, watching the first of the town workers arrive, happiness blooming across each of their faces as they witnessed what for them was nothing short of a miracle: the Angel Tree.

The instructions were simple, and by now the townsfolk knew them by heart. People in need should tie their wishes to the tree and those able to help should take those wishes and make them come true. A boy needing new basketball sneakers for the championship game would write down his request on a piece of paper, size and favorite colors included. Then he would carefully attach it to one of the springy branches of the tree. Those first few hours the boughs would remain empty. But then it would begin, the scraps of paper slowly cloaking the tree as though a swarm of white butterflies had stopped for a rest. Then over the next few days and weeks the scraps would dwindle down as helpers came and took off wishes, beginning the work of making them come true. Each year the Angel Tree brought great joy to the little town, felt by those who received much-needed help and those who could experience the singular pleasure of giving that help. Even those who merely witnessed the lives of their neighbors improve felt touched by the magic of the Angel Tree. It was a tradition the town looked forward to every year, holding its breath just the tiniest bit until that morning when the tree appeared, its presence as mysterious and wonderful as Christmas itself.

There were always those who boasted of plans to stake out the town square and discover who was behind the tree, of course. But in the end no one ever followed through. Even the most curious children knew that whoever was behind the Angel Tree wanted to keep their role a secret. And so it was that each year the Angel Tree appeared, wishes were made and granted, and the town of Pine River had just a little bit more to celebrate when Christmas arrived.

Until the year when everything changed.

Chapter 1

✳

Twenty-Two Days until Christmas

Lucy was shivering when she walked through the front door of her family's old Victorian house, her fingers icicles in the thick woolen gloves that she had knit for herself back in the fall. Though December in Pine River was always frigid, by now Lucy was used to it and knew to wear three layers, to always keep a hat pulled over her ears, and to walk fast. It was the last part that was the problem, though. Valentine could not walk fast and that meant that Lucy, who relied on the Seeing Eye dog to guide her wherever she needed to go, could not walk fast either.

Her parents had given Valentine to Lucy two years ago, on her ninth birthday. Her birthday was actually in

May but Valentine felt like the perfect name for the dog who had filled Lucy's heart. From the moment Lucy had first touched Valentine's velvety fur, feeling her new dog sniff her hand and then give it an affectionate nuzzle, Lucy had loved Valentine. Valentine was Lucy's independence, the ability to walk places on her own, to get through the halls of her school without worrying about stabbing someone in the shin with her walking stick.

But Valentine was more than Lucy's ticket to freedom. Lucy knew it was silly, but she secretly felt that Valentine was her best friend, the one she could tell anything and the one who was always there for her. And now, the way things were with her parents, the heavy silence from her normally too-chatty dad, the way her mother snapped over the tiniest things, the cloud of tension that had moved into the house like an unwanted house guest — well, now Lucy needed Valentine more than ever. Which was why it broke Lucy's heart that she couldn't be there for Valentine, not in the way her beloved dog needed.

"Lucy, hi, I didn't hear you come in," her dad said. He'd lost his job as an architect seven months ago, but it still felt weird to have him there when she got home in the afternoon. His steps were muffled as he walked into the front hall. He was probably wearing his old leather slippers that softened the sound of his steps on the hardwood floors. There were no rugs in the house because rugs could be a tripping hazard for a girl who could not see.

"Hi, Dad," Lucy said, trying to sound cheerful.

"How was your day, Sweetness?" he asked, gently rubbing her hair as she unlaced her boots. Sweetness was the nickname her parents had given her when they adopted her from China ten years before. When her birth mother had left her on the steps of a hospital under the cover of night, she had wrapped infant Lucy in a blanket, set her in a box, and put a sugared orange next to her. The women at the orphanage had explained to Lucy's parents that this meant she wished a life filled with good fortune and sweetness for her daughter, despite being unable to keep her. And Lucy's life *had* been sweet, mostly.

"It was a good day," Lucy said, searching for something interesting to tell her dad. "I think I did well on my quiz in English. And the school is collecting donations for Max Callahan and his family." Four weeks ago

DAPHNE BENEDIS-GRAB

Max, who was in sixth grade with Lucy at Pine River Middle School, had lost his home on Church Street in an electrical fire. "I was thinking I could knit them a couple of scarves and maybe some hats too." When Lucy was five her mom went on a kick to help Lucy find a hobby she could enjoy without her eyesight and knitting was the one that had stuck. Her mother helped break down patterns and pick out colors but Lucy's nimble fingers did the rest, turning out everything from gloves for her family to winter coats for Valentine. "I could even do gloves if Mom has a guess about what sizes might work."

"Great idea," her father said. "And I might have a football lying around somewhere that I could give to Max. He plays, doesn't he?"

"I think so," Lucy said. She and Max had a few classes together but weren't friends.

"Yeah, I'm pretty sure I've seen him out in Long Meadow Park with the flag team," her dad said. She heard the chair he was sitting on creak and a moment later Valentine let out a contented sigh. Her dad was probably rubbing the dog's belly, something she adored.

Lucy slid off her first boot, setting it carefully to the side of her seat so it wouldn't trip her when she stood up. Then she started on the second one.

"How's Valentine doing?" her dad asked cautiously. Her parents loved Valentine almost as much as Lucy did, which was part of what was making it all so hard.

"Um, okay I think," Lucy lied. Valentine was anything but okay.

"Did she slow you down?"

"No, it was fine." Lucy worked to get the boot off so she could escape this conversation. If there was nothing they could do, then there was no point in discussing Valentine's symptoms and how they were worsening.

Her dad was silent for a moment, and Lucy could hear that he had stopped petting Valentine. The boot was off and Lucy set it aside, then stood up. As she rose to her feet she could hear Valentine struggling to stand, the dog loyal to Lucy even now.

"Sweetness —" her dad said.

"Dad, I should start my homework," Lucy interrupted him, heading for the stairs that were a left turn and ten steps from where she had taken off her boots.

"Sweetness, I'm so sorry," her dad said, the chair creaking slightly as he, too, stood.

"Dad, it's not your fault," Lucy said.

Her father ruffled her hair again, then walked toward the kitchen with his slow, shuffling old-man gait while Lucy headed upstairs, waiting patiently for Valentine, who struggled to make it up the steps.

"Good girl," Lucy told her as they walked the fifteen steps to Lucy's bedroom. For the past two years she had not needed to know how many steps it was to anything, not when she had Valentine to guide her every move. But Lucy knew that she might need that information again, knowledge that twisted her chest into a tight knot.

In her room she heard Valentine pad over to her dog bed, the one her mother said was purple and the perfect complement to Valentine's rich brown fur. The labels *brown* and *purple* were not something Lucy, who had been blind her entire life, could imagine. But the words, like so many others, had their own texture and tenor and even their own taste in her mind. Purple was the sleekness of her satin bedspread, a low C ringing out from the piano, the soft sweetness of a banana. Brown was the warm down of her comforter, a bow drawn across the strings of a cello, the richness of chocolate-covered raisins.

Usually these images and the familiar sound of Valentine circling before settling down in her bed, calmed Lucy. But today calm was as far away as the place she had been born, and just as impossible to imagine. Because if something didn't change and change fast, these sounds would become a memory as well. Because Valentine, her beloved helper and companion and yes, her best friend, was dying. And her family did not have the money for the surgery and medication to save her.

Valentine had cancer. Burrowed into her soft fur was a tumor that was going to spread if it wasn't treated and wasn't treated fast. The vet, Dr. Lazarus, had been very optimistic about Valentine's chances. The cancer had been detected early and it was curable with surgery and follow-up chemotherapy. If they moved fast the vet was confident that Valentine could live a full, happy life. The problem, of course, was that surgery for a dog was expensive. Too expensive. Lucy's family simply did not have the thousands and thousands it would take to fully rid Valentine of the cancer. And so they were just treating the pain, hoping that the cancer would move slowly and Valentine could stay with them just a bit longer.

In any other place it would seem like a hopeless situation. But in the darkness of Lucy's deepest fears of losing her Valentine there was a thin ray of hope, golden and bright. The Angel Tree.

Lucy picked up the wish that she had already typed out with her voice-activated software and folded up tight, ready and waiting to be tied to one of the piney branches of the tree. It would go up any day now and when it did, Lucy was ready.

She only hoped it wouldn't be too late.

Chapter 2

---※---

Twenty-One Days
until Christmas

There were still a few last stars shining in the inky-blue sky when Max staggered out of his unfamiliar bed in the unfamiliar apartment that smelled like old boiled cauliflower. He groped his way down the dark hallway into the living room crammed with furniture, its wallpaper ripped and its ceiling criss-crossed with water stains. Max hated the run-down apartment that his family had been forced to move into after an electrical fire destroyed their home while they were off at school and work four weeks ago. All of them did. But as his dad kept pointing out, in the middle of a bitter Pine River winter they were lucky to have a roof over their heads.

The town had rallied around them, starting up collections and fund drives to help them move and to provide the family with the essentials — clothes and blankets and some toys for Max's little sister, Fiona. But what no one outside his family knew was that the expense of building or buying a new home was out of the Callahan family's price range, plain and simple. Which was why Max had been waking up well before the sun each day to check and see if the Angel Tree was up. He figured you had to get your wish up early if that wish was big. And the request for a house was about as big as it got.

Max peered sleepily through the window at the town square. In the dim splashes of light cast by the streetlights, he saw something that sent a current through his whole body, jolting him wide-awake: the Angel Tree.

For a moment Max just looked out at the tree, its branches swaying in the predawn wind. Then he ran to get dressed and grab the wish he had prepared two days after the fire.

The frigid air stung his face as he headed out of the building and made his way to the square but Max barely noticed. By the afternoon there would be over a hundred paths crisscrossing through the snow to the tree, but his was the first, his footsteps silent in the powdery snow covering the square. As he came closer to the tree, the zesty smell of pine mixed with the scent of doughnuts baking at Cinnamon Bakery across the way.

Max's hands were shaking from the cold as he carefully tied his wish, the very first wish, to a springy branch. He knew his wish was much too big. He was acting like little Fiona, who still believed in Santa Claus. But he fastened the wish to the tree anyway, letting go of the branch and hoping against hope that somehow, maybe, it might just come true.

Forty-five minutes later Max was headed out again, this time to school. As he passed the tree he saw that a few more tiny scraps of white paper had joined his against all that green.

"Hey, Max." He was pulled from his thoughts by his neighbor Lana Levkov who had come out of Cinnamon's with a big paper bag. Growing up, Max had always liked Lana, who could throw a football harder than most boys and always made the big kids let Max play even when they said he was too young. She'd left Pine River for college, but had moved back recently to take care of her mother, who had had a stroke. Lana was wearing a thick red wool coat and Max noticed a scrap of white paper in her hand.

"Hi," Max said. "Headed to the Angel Tree?"

Lana nodded. "It's a wish for my mom actually," she said. "She keeps talking about these Russian pastries she had when she was a girl. I can't make toast, let alone some complicated cream thing whose name my mom can't remember. But I figure someone in town will be able to figure it out and help us."

"Yeah," Max agreed. "I bet you're right." He'd never heard of a wish not coming true once it was hung on the tree. Though the wish he had put up that morning might be the first.

"I remember coming here when I was a girl," Lana said wistfully as she gazed at the tree. "Back then all I needed were simple things like horseback riding lessons and happiness was mine." She turned to Max. "I bet all you want is a new football and you'll be totally happy, right?"

Max did not know how to respond to such a dumb remark, so he just nodded, then headed toward Brewster Street.

There was nothing simple about Max's life. Not the wish he had hung on the tree that morning, not the place he was headed now. But even so, Max knew things were better now than they had been. Back in second grade — that had been the worst. That was when every other kid in his class had learned to read but Max could barely sound out the word *cat*. That was when he had become the class clown. Anytime a teacher called on him or he needed to share his work, Max pulled a prank instead. And while his school skills stayed awful, he became extremely good at pranks.

Midway through the year he was tested for learning disabilities. His stomach twisted up when he thought of that awful test, of how the clock had ticked on for an eternity but it still hadn't been enough time for him to get through all the problems. Still, after that he had finally gotten the help he needed and slowly got back on track, though not fast enough. He had had to repeat second grade, the most humiliating thing imaginable. If it weren't for his best friend, Cami, giving the evil eye to anyone who even looked like they might tease him, Max might have become the first second-grade dropout in the history of Pine River Elementary School. Instead, he stepped up the pranks, earning a reputation that bordered on being legendary.

"Max, what's up!" his friend Alec shouted. Max turned around and felt the shocking cold of a snowball hit him smack in the face. Chunks of ice slid down his cheeks and he rubbed his eyes quickly to clear them. Alec, Danny, and Lucas, friends from the flag football team, were half a block behind him hooting with laughter.

"You're dead!" Max shouted, scooping up a handful of snow and lunging toward them.

"It's on!" Lucas yelled, mashing a pile of snow into a tight ball as he ran across the street. Max ducked behind a tree as Danny sent another snowball flying. Then he charged. They were a block from school now and the kids walking toward the big brick building either ran to get out of the way or began digging into the snow for their own artillery. Soon the area was a mass of flying snow, the air alive with screams — and then the inevitable whistle as the vice principal broke up the battle and herded everyone into the building.

Max was wet and his heart was pumping but he was grinning as he headed up the steps with his friends. A snowball fight was definitely a good start to the day.

"You throw like a wimp," Alec said cheerfully as they walked into the heated hallways of Pine River Middle School. Speckled gray rugs had been set out over the floors to absorb the slush tracked in and the faded cream-colored walls were papered with posters for various clubs, meetings, and games.

"At least I don't throw like your mama," Max replied. Though it wasn't one of his strongest comebacks, Alec snickered and high-fived Max. "Your mama" jokes were a favorite form of communication for the team.

The warning bell rang and Max headed for his locker, greeting people as he went. As he walked past Joe Thompson's locker, Max could see Joe glaring at him. Joe had been new at the start of the year, a pale, skinny kid with shaggy brown hair who walked with his head down.

On the second day of school Max had stopped by Joe's locker to ask him if he'd want to join the flag football team. Joe hadn't seemed too into the idea, but Max had figured he was probably shy. When Max had made a few jokes, trying to loosen him up, Joe had hauled off and punched him. Max had been so shocked he hadn't even thought to punch Joe back. He had just stood there, blood dripping from his nose, the gasps of his classmates in his ears as the new kid stalked off.

Of course he hadn't told any of the teachers who asked about his bloody face what had happened. Max was not a snitch. But he did regret that he had just stood there, not even giving Joe a shove before he walked away.

In the end, though, Joe's obnoxious attitude and the fact that he had punched Max for no reason had combined to make him the most hated kid at Pine River. Not that he even seemed to notice. He kept to himself, ignoring everyone. The only time he ever reacted was when Max passed. Then he acted like Max was some kind of monster.

"Hey, Max, I'm desperate," said Tom, another friend from the flag football team, as he pushed through the crowded hall and threw an arm across Max's shoulders. "You're my only hope, Obi-Wan."

Max always appreciated a reference to Star Wars. "What's up?" he asked.

"Ms. Rehfisch is giving us a quiz and I didn't have time to study," Tom said as they turned the corner and arrived at Max's locker. "If I flunk it, my parents will ground me and then I'll miss the game on Sunday." Every

Sunday there was a pickup ice hockey game on the river that neither Max nor Tom ever missed. "You've got to do something to stop that quiz."

Tom needed a prank pulled off. Of course. That was the kind of "help" people came to Max for, the one thing he was known for. Which used to make Max puff with pride but somehow lately was making him feel trapped in a box, the edges pressing tight against him. "You've come to the right place, young Jedi," he said, shrugging it off. "I'm on it."

"Excellent," Tom said, slapping him on the back and heading down the hall.

Max watched him for a moment, then began shoving stuff in his locker as the bell rang. He slammed the metal door shut with a clank and jogged down the hall, his thoughts drifting back to the quiet dark of the morning and the wish that he knew could never come true.

Chapter 3

---※---

Twenty-One Days
until Christmas

"H e's such a jerk."

The words were whispered but Joe heard them as he walked past, just like he was supposed to. Everyone at Pine River Middle School hated him and they wanted him to know it. And he did, he knew it. But the thing was, he didn't care. Joe had not come to Pine River to make friends. He had come here because he had to. It was his duty.

Though the steamy hallway of Pine River Middle School was packed with students ready to head home after the last bell, a path seemed to open up for Joe as he headed to his locker. It was kind of funny because he was probably the one person at the school who didn't have anywhere better to go. Everyone else had clubs, plans with friends, lessons, or even just a home to go to. But Joe was camped out with his uncle Leon, in a small one-bedroom apartment. The first night, Leon had unfurled a sleeping bag for Joe and told him to "park it wherever it fits." It fit next to the dining room table, so that was where Joe stretched out each night, the wood floor hard under the knobs of his spine.

He turned a corner, almost bumping into Anya and Lucy, who were both in sixth grade too. Joe didn't know too many people at the school, but a small blind girl with a chocolate Lab as a Seeing Eye dog were hard to miss. Anya glared at Joe as though he had purposefully tried to trip Lucy, then swept past with a curl of her lip.

Back home Joe hadn't been one of the popular kids, but he'd had a group of friends to sit with at lunch and hang around with after school. And everyone else had pretty much just left him alone. Being hated like this was new. But in those first awful weeks at Pine River Middle School, Joe's insides were twisted so tight he could barely get through the school day. The effort it would have taken to make friends was as far out of reach as the sun. When the fight with Max happened, Joe's fate as school outcast had been sealed. Joe couldn't let it get to him though. If kids in a small town that was not his real home didn't like him, well, he could live with that. He had bigger things to worry about.

Joe stopped at his locker toward the end of the main hall and began to spin through the combination. Then, behind him, he heard the one voice at Pine River Middle School that made him react.

"It was amazing, I'm telling you," Max drawled, his voice carrying down the hall. Joe snuck a look out of the corner of his eye. The three girls with Max were hanging on his every word.

Joe's stomach burned as Max went past, boasting about some prank he had pulled off in his English class. Everyone thought Max's jokes were funny — everyone but Joe that is.

Then Max was gone, swallowed up in the crowd that was headed out into the frigid afternoon. And the burning in Joe's gut cooled.

"Have a good night."

Joe looked up, surprised. It was Camilla, the girl with the locker next to him. She had skin the color of the milky coffee his mom drank and her hair hung down in hundreds of braids, each ending in a pink, silver, or gold bead. They clinked together musically whenever Camilla tossed her head, though even Joe knew that the real music Camilla made was with the violin. Everyone loved hearing her play at assemblies and town events. Camilla was the one person at school who was friendly to Joe, smiling and sometimes, like today, actually saying something to him. Something nice.

Joe nodded as Camilla headed down the hall. Sure he could have tried to start a conversation but it just felt like too little too late. His status was set, so why try to change it?

He finished packing up his book bag, then hoisted it over one shoulder and shut his locker. He looked out the window at the end of the hall and saw that it was snowing yet again. He pulled on his coat — meant for the mild winters of Virginia, it barely helped, and he froze every time he went outside — and then hesitated. It was tempting to stay warm just a little bit longer. So he headed to the one place he was actually welcome at Pine River Middle School: the library.

Back home in Virginia, Joe had been on the cross-country team, played in the chess club, and always worked up a complicated project for the science fair with his friend Louis. But the thing he loved most was reading, probably because his mom made such a big thing about their weekly trips to the library and the time they spent reading together after dinner every night. Here in Pine River there was no cross-country and Joe knew he wasn't welcome in any clubs, not that he'd want to join anyway. So he spent most of his free time reading, making him a regular at the big, welcoming school library.

The halls had pretty much emptied out as Joe headed toward the east wing of the building, coughing a bit as he went. He stopped for a drink at the fountain just outside the library, to soothe his throat, then walked through into the library.

The large room was lined with row after row of tall wooden bookcases. In the center were matching wooden worktables and the big circulation desk run by Ms. Marwich, the librarian. Ms. Marwich seemed ancient to Joe, with her old-fashioned clothes and the white hair she wore tucked up in a bun. Still, she had more energy than almost anyone Joe knew, and she was always happy to see any student who walked through the doors. Even the most hated student in the school: Joe himself.

Today she was checking books back in and she looked up, her blue eyes crinkling with pleasure when Joe came over. "Joe, so nice to see you," she said. "How are you?"

Joe cleared his throat. "Okay."

"Here, let me get something for you," she said, pushing aside framed pictures of her wedding day and her cat, Tango, and rummaging through the papers and books that covered her desk. After a moment she came up with a cough drop. "That cough just isn't leaving you alone, is it?"

"Thanks," Joe said, unwrapping the cherry lozenge and putting it in his mouth. It was a lot more soothing than the cold water had been.

"Some friends of mine own the town drugstore," Ms. Marwich said. "A lovely older couple — the VonWolfs. They're mostly retired but everyone who works there is helpful. You should stop by on your way home and stock up on some of these." She passed him a few more lozenges, which Joe slipped into his pocket.

"Okay," Joe said, though he really didn't have extra money to spare on cough drops. It wasn't like he was really sick — it was just a cough.

"Tell the VonWolfs Rona sent you," Ms. Marwich said with a wink. "They give special deals to my friends."

It was kind of pathetic but this was the first time anyone in Pine River had called Joe a friend.

"So what are your plans for Christmas?" Ms. Marwich asked.

Joe stiffened. Christmas was something he most definitely didn't want to think about. But Ms. Marwich was looking at him and he had to say something so he pushed the cough drop to the side of his mouth. "Not much."

Ms. Marwich's brow furrowed. "What do you mean? Christmas is such a special time of year. Your family must be planning something." Ms. Marwich, like everyone else in Pine River, had no idea about Joe's family situation and Joe aimed to keep it that way.

"I'm sure we'll do something," he said, trying to sound nonchalant. "It's not a big deal." It was such a lie that the words were hard to force out.

And clearly Ms. Marwich could see he wasn't telling the truth because her brow furrowed even more. "Christmas is a big deal," she said gently.

At that Joe could only shrug and look away.

"It sounds like you could use the Angel Tree," Ms. Marwich said after a moment.

Joe's eyebrow scrunched. "What?" he asked.

Ms. Marwich explained how it worked, and Joe had to admit it was kind of impressive the way the people in Pine River helped each other out. But it didn't all fit.

"What if a kid who lives in an apartment building asks for a pony?" Joe asked.

Ms. Marwich pressed her fingertips together. "Hm, that happened a few years back," she said. "People get creative. Let's see, I think that girl got to go to a riding camp in the summer."

"Oh, that makes sense," Joe said.

"It seems to me that maybe you have a wish or two that might need granting," Ms. Marwich went on. "You should give the Angel Tree a try."

"I don't think so," Joe said, shaking his head. The tree was there for the people who called Pine River home, not for someone like him who was hated by everyone. But even as he thought that, he could feel his wish growing, filling up his whole stomach with how much he wanted it.

Ms. Marwich looked at him for a moment. "That tree is there for everyone," she said softly. "And the wishes on it are about people needing some help and other people being able to offer that help. It's simple, really, and it's the spirit of the holiday. Christmas has been my favorite holiday since I was a girl — and even more so now that Pine River has the Angel Tree."

It was his mother's favorite holiday too. "I'm not sure," Joe said. It seemed silly to even hope someone would choose to help him.

"Well, I am," Ms. Marwich said firmly, handing him a pen and paper. "You don't have to tell me or any-one else what you're wishing for. Just write it up and run along. The Angel Tree is waiting."

Joe shrugged. He didn't want to argue, even though it would probably come to nothing. He scribbled his wish on the paper and waved to Ms. Marwich as he headed out.

It was a short but frigid walk into town. The snow had stopped, but wind gusted through his thin coat, spread-ing icy fingers over his skin. He stopped at Tasty Market to pick up a can of soup for dinner and then headed to the center of Pine River. The old brick buildings flank-ing the square were covered in fresh snow and lit up with strings of Christmas lights. Snow was piled in mounds across the square and the Angel Tree towered above, the deep green boughs sparkling with tiny colored lights and covered with white paper wishes.

Joe's footsteps were muffled by the snow as he waded over. The tree was huge. He gazed up at it, the branches rustling in the wind, the top of the tree seeming to touch the stars that were just beginning to appear in the satiny-blue sky. There *was* something magical about it, he thought as he tied on his wish, something that made him believe that maybe, just maybe, the wish he so desperately longed for really would come true.

Chapter 4

*Twenty Days
until Christmas*

H ey, Cami!"

Cami turned, brushing a few stray braids out of her face, and saw her friend Oliver, his sax case tucked under one arm, loping to catch up to her. The final bell had just rung, meaning it was Cami's favorite time of day: orchestra rehearsal.

"What's up?" Cami asked, shifting her backpack so she could hold her violin case more carefully.

"Not much," Oliver said, falling in step with her. "Have you started practicing your solo for the Christmas Gala?"

Cami couldn't help feeling a glow at the mention of the solo. She had been thrilled when the conductor, Mr.

Carmichael, had given it to her last week. But her grand-mother was always telling her to be humble, so she tried to look modest as she nodded. "Yeah. It's hard but hope-fully I'll be ready for the Gala."

Oliver laughed. "You probably have the whole thing down already."

Cami shrugged. It was true that she'd spent the entire weekend memorizing and perfecting the piece, a section of Handel's *Messiah*. If the Gala was that very night, she'd probably be ready.

They were nearing the orchestra room and the sounds of middle school musicians beginning to warm up echoed through the hall. Cami was eager to join them, but just as they got to the door she noticed her friend Max walk-ing down the hall, probably heading to detention. The pranks he pulled were funny but Cami wasn't sure they were worth all the time he spent paying for them.

"I'll see you in a second," she said to Oliver, then waved at Max, who grinned when he saw her.

"How's it going?" he asked, shoving his shaggy black hair out of his face. Max always needed a haircut.

"Good," she said. "How are you?" She tried to sound casual but Max knew her well.

"I'm fine, don't worry," he said, rolling his eyes.

Cami did worry, though. Sure Max was a popular middle schooler now, but she remembered when he was the kid who had to repeat second grade, the one everyone made jokes about. She'd watched after him like a hawk, not letting anyone get away with teasing him until everyone realized it was a lot more fun to laugh with Max and his pranks, than at him. And now, with the fire at his house a few weeks ago, and the endless detentions, Cami couldn't help feeling concerned for her friend again.

"I know the school is collecting more stuff for your family but is there anything else you guys need?" she asked. "Bigger stuff like furniture? Because my grandmother was saying she could help organize another collection through our church."

Max shook his head. "The apartment is too small for any more furniture."

Cami hated seeing the way the corners of his mouth turned down and she searched for a subject that might cheer him up.

"Do you have a wish for the Angel Tree?" she asked. Everyone in town loved talking about their beloved Christmas tradition.

Max glanced down the hall where some boys were tossing a football. Cami figured they had about two more minutes before a teacher caught them. "Not really," he said. "How about you?"

Cami nodded. "I want some rosin, a new chin rest, and a couple of new music books." Nothing on her list was all that expensive but Cami and her grandmother always had to watch their spending, and Cami knew the Angel Tree gifts helped a lot.

"Getting ready for Carnagale Hall," Max said, his usual cheer back in his voice.

"Carnegie," Cami corrected, then grinned. "Hopefully one of these days." She didn't have to be humble with Max — he knew how much she loved her violin, how exhilarating it was to have music flowing through her fingertips, how hard she worked. "Speaking of which, I should get to rehearsal."

"See you later," Max said, heading toward the guys playing catch.

"Don't get in trouble," Cami called, but of course it was too late and Max was already jumping up to grab a pass.

Cami shook her head as she walked into the orchestra

room, but then the sounds and smells pulled her in and soon Cami was lost in the familiar joy of making music.

The sky was darkening as Cami walked up the front path to the little house she had shared with her grandmother ever since her parents had died in a car crash when she was a baby. Cami had no memories of her parents but her grandmother had more than made up for that, attending every concert Cami ever played in, spending hours planning the perfect birthday party every year, and having a knack for knowing exactly when Cami needed a good pep talk or special pancake breakfast to lift her spirits.

As she slid the key into the front door, Cami had the delicious wrung-out feeling that only came after a good long session with her violin. She especially loved the Christmas pieces the band was preparing for the Pine River Christmas Gala and of course, her solo. She was humming one of the tunes as she closed the front door, but then she heard her grandmother talking on the phone in the kitchen. Her grandmother spoke to her daughter,

Cami's aunt Aisha, at least once a week and it sounded like they were going over the menu for Christmas dinner. So Cami quietly took off her boots — sound traveled well in their tiny home — and was heading up the stairs when she heard her name.

"Yes, of course I wish Cami was more like that," her grandmother said. "Willa is just so poised and focused on the things that matter in life."

Cami froze. Her cousin Willa was two years older than Cami and the shining star of the family. She got straight As, was captain of the chess club, a top member of the Mathletes, and had recently begun to volunteer at the hospital near their house in Pittsburgh. Cancer didn't have a chance now that the mighty Willa was going after it.

"Cami's always off playing her violin," her grandmother went on with a dismissive sniff. "Instead of being practical and helpful, like Willa . . . Mmhmm . . . I'm sure she'll grow up sometime. I just hope that time comes sooner than later."

Cami sank down on the stairs. She leaned her pounding forehead against the bannister and tried to wrap her mind around what she had just overheard. Of course

Cami had always known she wasn't like the rest of her family. She was pretty much the opposite of her practical grandmother, an ex-accountant who kept a clean house, cooked healthy, economical meals, and wore rain boots if there was a single cloud in the sky. And she was nothing like her no-nonsense aunt Aisha, a hard-working lawyer, or perfect Willa. Cami was the artist and she had always felt a bit proud of that.

But now Cami had heard the truth about what her grandmother thought and suddenly everything she'd been devoted to felt silly, like a kid believing Disneyland was the real world.

Cami looked at her violin case and a feeling of shame crept over her. Was her music just a stupid childish thing? Maybe she did need to change, to grow up, as her grandmother said. And maybe the time to do that was now.

Chapter 5

✳

Twenty Days until Christmas

L ucy had gone to the Angel Tree the second school let out on Thursday, her wish clutched in her hand, the snow falling softly on her face as she secured the paper to a springy branch, breathing in the smell of pine in the quiet square. She knew her wish was a lot to ask at a time when so many Pine River families were struggling to get by. Perhaps even too much. Lucy wasn't sure. The one thing she did know was that her beloved pet was running out of time.

She could feel it in her bones as she and Valentine trudged home on Friday afternoon. Her dog was moving slower than ever.

And then suddenly, on the sidewalk along Main Street, Valentine stumbled slightly and let out a small bark. Lucy tried to stay calm, but panic made it hard to breathe as she ripped off her gloves and ran her hands over the dog's soft fur, taking special care to see if something had gotten stuck in one of her paws.

"Is everything okay, Lucy?"

Lucy recognized the musical voice of Alma Sanchez, one of the people who organized town events like the Christmas Gala.

"I'm not sure," Lucy said. There was a sweet trickle of relief knowing that a grown-up she trusted, who could see, was there to help. But her hands were shaking as she stood up. "I think something hurt Valentine but I can't figure out what."

"Let's take a look," Ms. Sanchez said calmly, her coat rustling as she knelt down next to Valentine. "What do you say, sweet girl, can I take a look at you?"

Lucy liked how Ms. Sanchez talked to Valentine, but she couldn't help noticing that Valentine didn't thump her tail in response. Valentine always thumped her tail happily when people spoke to her.

"Hm, I can't find anything," Ms. Sanchez said after

a moment. "Everything seems to be fine. Do you think perhaps she just tripped and it surprised her?"

Lucy knew that was not the case but to tell Ms. Sanchez the truth, to put into words the fear that now gripped her with iron strong fingers, was more than she could bear. "Yes, I'm sure that's it," she said.

"Can I help you with anything else?" Ms. Sanchez asked.

"No, but thank you," Lucy said. She picked up Valentine's lead in her shaky hands and headed home. Ms. Sanchez's words had confirmed Lucy's fears. The yelp of pain did not have to do with an injury. It was from the illness. Valentine was starting to suffer from the disease that was going to take her away from Lucy forever.

As they walked, Lucy murmured words of comfort to Valentine, even though she could barely hold herself together. The important thing was to get Valentine home and then have her parents call the vet to see what could be done to ease Valentine's pain. The one crucial thing the whole family had agreed upon was that they must be sure Valentine never, ever suffered. So Lucy did not, could not, think about what it might mean if the vet was unable to stop the pain that had made Valentine whimper on their walk home.

The thing she clung to as they slowly made their way home was the Angel Tree. Now, more than ever, she needed her wish to come true.

Lucy slowly followed Valentine up the wooden porch steps and jiggled the key in the sticky lock of their heavy front door. When it swung open, an unusual fragrance greeted her. Under the normal aromas of orange all-purpose cleaner and freshly dried laundry, mixed with the scent of a chicken roasting in the oven for dinner, were the sharp smell of disinfectant and the sweet fragrance of perfume. And Lucy's mother did not wear perfume.

"Lucy, is that you?" her dad called. "There's a wonderful surprise."

Lucy's heart was suddenly racing in her chest. The perfume could be anyone but disinfectant — that would mean a doctor or —

"It's Dr. Lazarus with incredible news," her father went on. "She's here to pick up Valentine for her surgery first thing tomorrow morning. It's all been taken care of — the surgery, the medication, everything."

Lucy's throat was too thick to speak and tears ran down her face. She knelt down and hugged Valentine, who licked the tears of joy from Lucy's cheeks.

Her dad bent down and rubbed Lucy's back. "Dr. Lazarus says we're well within the time frame to save Valentine. She's going to need a week or so to recover from the surgery and then we'll need to give her chemo pills. Luckily, the chemo doesn't usually affect pets the way it affects humans, so we can hope that Valentine won't experience any side effects. . . ." He must have noticed that Lucy was too overwhelmed to absorb any of the details. "She's going to be fine, Sweetness. Valentine is going to be with us for a long time to come."

Lucy struggled to her feet. "Thank you," she said, though the words didn't begin to express how grateful she was.

"It's one of the angels who deserves your thanks," the vet said, resting a gentle hand on Lucy's shoulder. "One of them plucked your wish from the Angel Tree and came by my office first thing this morning to set everything up. And your dad is right, Lucy: Valentine is going to be better than ever once we get that tumor out of her."

Lucy helped Dr. Lazarus and her father load Valentine into a travel crate and then listened as they discussed final details.

"The tumor is close enough to the surface that the surgery is not hugely invasive," Dr. Lazarus said as she put on her coat and readied for the trip to her office just outside town. "So the recovery should be fast. We'll have her on a precautionary antibiotic and, of course, the chemo pills. You'll need to get those from the drugstore but I've already put in the first order and the VonWolfs will have everything you need by tomorrow. And you should be able to pick Valentine up Monday afternoon!"

The information washed over Lucy as she crouched, petting Valentine through the slats of the crate.

"All right, we're ready to roll," Dr. Lazarus said.

Lucy gave her dog's wet nose an extra little pat. "Dr. Lazarus is going to make you better," she whispered to Valentine, who gave a short bark of protest at being shut in the crate.

Lucy laughed. "Don't worry, Valentine, you'll be out of there and back home before you know it." The words were like honey on her tongue.

Lucy's dad helped the vet roll the crate down to the car and then load it in the trunk. Lucy heard the purr of the engine and the crunch of the tires over the frozen driveway.

"My wish came true," Lucy said. She thought of the candied orange her birth mother had given her, and the sweetness and good fortune that had come to visit her. She thought of her dog tucked safely in the vet's car, nearing the office where her disease would be cured. And she thought of the next weeks and months and even years that she would now be able to share with her treasured dog.

But mostly she thought about the Angel Tree and how incredibly grateful she was for the wondrous gift it had given her.

Chapter 6

Eighteen Days until Christmas

T he night Cami overheard what her grandmother really thought of her violin, she'd lain awake in the quiet dark of her bedroom, restless and miserable. She'd thought about saying something to her grandmother, but she felt too hurt to even know where to begin. Then, sometime around midnight, she'd come to a decision: She was not going to be the fool of her family, the one who wasted time playing a silly instrument while Willa helped doctors find a cure for cancer and heart attacks and whatever other practical, helpful things she did at the hospital. The old Cami who wasted hours practicing was gone and a new Cami was coming to town, a Cami even more helpful and practical than Willa herself.

It was just a question of making a few changes.

The first step was the hardest: getting rid of her violin. But she'd done it. Saturday morning she had headed to the town pawnshop, Second Comings, violin in hand. When she'd entered the musty but cozy store, part of her had not believed that Yasmine Tennyson, who ran the shop, would actually take her violin. But after hesitating, the shop owner had agreed. In fact, that very afternoon she had called Cami to say that the violin had sold. Cami was unprepared, both for the sale and for the sickening feeling of regret that had flooded over her. But it had been too late to call things off.

Now Cami kept reminding herself that this was for the best. She had gone into the store and collected her money, using it to buy practical, Willa-like gifts for her grandmother's Christmas presents. Now all she had to do was find a project, something truly spectacular to show her grandmother just how focused and helpful she was.

That Sunday night Cami helped her grandmother prepare their dinner of pork chops, green beans, and fresh-baked biscuits, and set the table without being asked.

"My, you're a help tonight," her grandmother commented after they had said grace.

"I want to do more around the house," Cami said. She figured if she wanted to be useful, her own home was a good place to start. Plus she'd start to go slightly crazy sitting in her room alone, missing her violin.

"That sounds lovely," Cami's grandmother said, but Cami noticed her frowning a bit as she passed Cami the platter of pork chops. It was probably because Cami wasn't exactly the best kitchen helper. Thanks to her the beans were limp and overcooked and the biscuits had nearly burned. But she'd get better with practice, and her grandmother would be happy to have her help. So happy she might even want to boast about it to Aunt Aisha.

"I didn't hear you practicing," her grandmother said as she neatly sliced a section of pork chop into bite-size chunks.

The words cut into Cami now that she knew her grandmother's true feelings about her violin. "I'm taking a bit of a break from violin," Cami said. "I want to focus on other things." She would wait until Christmas, when she had given her grandmother all the gifts she had bought, to tell her the violin was gone.

Her grandmother's brow furrowed. "What other things?" she asked.

"Well, I want to bring my grades up," Cami said. "See if I can get all As. And maybe I'll start playing chess."

Her grandmother was staring at her like an alien had taken over Cami's body. "You? The girl who 'accidentally' knocked the board off the table when your cousin tried to teach you to play, *you* play chess?"

Well. This was not the reaction Cami had been hoping for. "I'm older now," she informed her grandmother loftily. "I can see all the benefits of chess now."

Her grandmother raised an eyebrow. "And just what would those benefits be?"

Cami couldn't think of a single positive thing about chess, but she was saved by the ringing phone and her grandmother's heated indignation at telemarketers calling during the dinner hour. As her grandmother slammed the phone down and launched into a rant, Cami's thoughts drifted back to the fact that she needed to find a way to do something really, truly helpful, like Willa and the hospital. Something that would have her grandmother boasting to everyone in town about what a responsible, helpful granddaughter she had. Something better than limp green beans.

Later that night Cami went down to kiss her grandmother before bed. She was peering at her email, her bifocals low on her nose. It always cracked Cami up to see her old-fashioned grandmother at the computer, but her grandmother liked to keep "current" and was an active member of her church's online community and a regular at online mah-jongg.

She was smiling as Cami walked over. "I just heard the nicest thing," she said, clicking off the computer and taking off her glasses. "You remember how poor Julia Whittaker had decided she needed to find a new home for Pebbles because her arthritis is just too bad to take him out every day for walks?"

Hm, Cami must have missed that. To be honest, she often tuned things out because she was running through pieces of music in her head. But she nodded anyway, wondering if maybe she could offer to walk Pebbles. That would be fun. Except for the cleaning up poop part.

"Well, her son put a wish up on the Angel Tree, asking for a dog walker so that Julia could keep her dog," her grandmother said. "And just a day later a nice high school student came knocking on her door, ready to take old Pebbles out for a romp. He's been hired permanently by one of the angels."

"That's great," Cami said, a little disappointed to lose her opportunity to help, though a little relieved too.

"That Angel Tree is a godsend," her grandmother said, standing up and stretching a little. "Whoever is behind it sure is doing something wonderful for our town."

"Remember how when I was little I thought Santa set it up? I believed that for years." Cami twisted one of her braids around her fingers. "Who do you think it really is?"

"Well, that's the mystery of it, isn't it," her grandmother said, heading to the kitchen for her nightly cup of peppermint tea. "But there sure are a lot of people who would like to give him or a her a hearty thanks."

Cami froze. That was it! That was what she could do to help! She could find the person who was behind the

Angel Tree. Maybe she could get Max to help. And together they could arrange the biggest, best town-wide thank-you that had ever been.

And *that* would have her grandmother bursting with pride.

Chapter 7

Seventeen Days
until Christmas

Joe was in a good mood as he headed down the hall of Pine River Middle School. The night before, Leon had allowed Joe to use his laptop for three hours. Joe had logged in immediately and spent the night playing online chess with Ariana, his closest friend from chess club back home in Virginia. They had IMed a little too, but when she kept asking about his new friends and if he had joined the chess club in Pine River, which she mistakenly called his new home, Joe had put all his energy into the game.

A group of jock guys ran past, one bumping hard enough against Joe to cause him to stumble back. The guy's friend high-fived him, just in case Joe thought that it had been an accident. Joe squared his shoulders and pulled his thoughts from the fun of the night before. Instead he focused on getting down the hall without suffering any more bodily harm.

Once he reached his locker, he pulled out his books for his morning class, then checked the cell phone that he kept in the pocket of his backpack, the one that was only used in emergencies. He expected to see the usual picture of him and his mom at Virginia Beach that was his screen saver. But when the phone lit up, it showed that he had a message waiting.

A cold sweat broke out on Joe's forehead as he stared at the screen. It was possible that this was nothing, a telemarketer or a wrong number. But there was a chance that this was the call Joe had been dreading, confirming the fear that had hung over him like a thick fog every day since his mother had left.

This was how it was when the one parent you had was a United States Marine, putting her life in danger every day to serve the country she loved. Joe's hands were shaky as he dialed his voice mail.

"Hi, Love, it's me." Joe let out a long sigh of relief at his mom's cheerful voice. "And I have the most wonderful news! You know how disappointed I was that we didn't have the money for me to come home for Christmas. I hated the thought of being apart on our favorite holiday. But the most amazing thing has happened — a miracle really! I'm coming home for Christmas. An anonymous donor — something about an angel — called up the Marine Travel Office and made arrangements for me to fly straight to Pittsburgh. There's a rental car waiting in my name and apparently the drive to Pine River is a quick ninety minutes north. So I'll be there before the clock strikes midnight on Christmas Eve." Her voice was choked up as she spoke the last words. "I'll be with you, my darling boy, we'll be together for Christmas." The message clicked off and Joe blinked back tears.

"The Angel Tree," Joe whispered. When he had tied his wish to celebrate Christmas with his mom to the tree a few days ago, he hadn't even allowed himself to hope that it might come true. But incredibly enough, it had. He would be together with his mother at Christmas, the one thing he wanted more than anything. His mother was right: It *was* a miracle and the best Christmas present ever.

"Hey, Joe," Cami said, closing her locker and smiling at him.

Joe looked at her and beamed, joy from the message shining across his face.

Cami stepped back looking shocked. "That's the first time you've ever smiled at me," she said.

Joe realized it might be the first time he had smiled since he arrived in Pine River. And the first time he was thankful to be here, in a place where wishes really did come true.

Chapter 8

Seventeen Days
until Christmas

O kay, class, let's settle down and get ready to see, up close and personal, the effects of global warming on the Antarctic penguin." Mr. Woodward gave Max a solemn nod. Max saluted, then flicked off the science classroom's lights. He saw Sameera and Liz roll their eyes. Liz sank down on her seat, clearly ready to use the class movie time to take a nap.

But she needn't have been worried about being bored: Max had seen to that.

Mr. Woodward pressed PLAY on the ancient class DVD player, then walked to the back of the room with his arms folded. Just to ensure the fun lasted as long as possible, Max made sure to push his chair out so it was blocking the aisle and Mr. Woodward's best path back to the DVD player.

The screen at the front of the classroom was dark for a moment and then, instead of some depressing film about dying penguins, the screen was lit up with a bright title: *The Miracle of Life*.

"It's a miracle!" someone shouted.

Energy coursed across the classroom. A group of guys cheered, and the girls shrieked and covered their faces as the DVD Max had grabbed from the eighth-grade health class bin in the AV room began.

Mr. Woodward rushed toward the front of the class-room but caught his foot on the edge of Max's chair, and tripped.

"What do you know about reproduction?" a smiling nurse asked, staring into the camera.

Several boys shouted responses at once as Mr. Woodward untangled his feet and finally made it to the DVD player. He hit the OFF button so hard the machine fell and crashed onto the floor. "Liz, get the lights," he shouted.

Once Liz had flicked the lights on, Max could see that his teacher's face was red and he was glaring straight at Max. He pointed to the door. "Principal, now," he snapped.

Max didn't even bother protesting. After all, who but him would have thought to grab the DVD when the AV room was left open by mistake, and then get to class early enough to swap out the discs?

The class began chanting his name as Max, in a blaze of glory, headed out the door.

Max was stuffing books in his backpack when he heard his name later that afternoon.

"Max, that was too funny," Sameera called across the crowded hall. The final bell had rung and everyone was eager to get outside.

Max grinned as Sameera elbowed her way over, Liz following in her wake.

"I thought Mr. Woodward was going to burst a blood vessel," Sameera went on.

"He was so mad," Liz agreed, giggling as she smoothed her long brown hair.

A sliver of guilt jabbed Max at the memory of his teacher's dismay.

"Did you get in a lot of trouble?" Sameera asked, her face a mask of concern but her eyes lit up, eager for gory details.

Max leaned against his locker, his eyes downcast. "Ms. Sato doesn't know what to do with me," he said with mock sadness. "I'm just a lost cause."

In reality Ms. Sato had a lot of ideas of what to do with Max and none of them were particularly appealing. He'd been given the usual detention, the call home to his parents, and a lecture about how his behavior impacted his learning as well as the people around him. "Do you think your parents really want to be hearing from me now?" Ms. Sato had asked, in her sharp, straightforward way.

"No, ma'am," Max had said. Sitting in her office, Max had felt a little like a lost cause. Ms. Sato was right — his parents were dealing with the loss of their home and the fact that their insurance wouldn't cover all the costs of a new house. They did not need calls about Max getting in trouble yet again.

But this was who Max was: the kid who pulled off pranks and made the long school day more interesting. And standing here now, under the admiring gazes of

Sameera and Liz, it was impossible to imagine being anything else.

"You guys, look!"

The three of them turned to see Olivia, the third member of the girls' trio, rushing over, a big box in her arms.

"What is that?" Liz asked.

"My Angel Tree wish," Olivia crowed. "It came true already!"

"Wow, that was fast," Max said.

Sameera was frowning. "That's not your wish," she said.

"Yeah, I thought you asked for a dress to wear to the Christmas Gala," Liz agreed, eyeing the box. It looked to Max like it was perfectly capable of holding a dress but the girls seemed certain it did not.

"No, it's a million times better," Olivia explained, setting the box down and opening the top with a flourish. "It's a compact sewing machine!"

"No way!" Sameera squealed, clapping her hands together.

Max stepped back as the three of them began shrieking in an alarming manner over the gift but he got why they were so excited. Olivia was the queen of do-it-yourself stuff, from the scarves and hats she crocheted to the tiny cupcakes she baked for birthdays. Max didn't know why you'd bother making a hat when you could just buy one, but the cupcakes were really good and Olivia clearly liked making stuff. If there was anyone better suited to start sewing her own clothes, Max couldn't think of who it was. That was the thing about the Angel Tree — the people who gave the gifts really knew the recipients and figured out the ultimate way to make the wish come true.

For a second he thought of his own wish, but in the light of day he knew there was no way it could ever come true. He'd been dumb to put it up in the first place.

"Look, there are even some patterns to get me started," Olivia said, holding up a pile of papers. The top one had measurements and lines that looked like high-level algebra to Max but he glanced at it to be polite. It was copied from a book called *Create the Dress, Create Yourself*, which seemed like the stupidest title ever to Max. The girls seemed unfazed by it, though, instead going on about styles and fit.

Max tuned out and went back to piling books in his backpack. He was pretty sure he had everything but still double-checked the homework organizer Zoe had given him at the beginning of the year. Sure enough he'd forgotten his math book, so he rummaged around his locker for it, then stuffed it in on top.

"So, Max, where are you headed?" Sameera asked as he slammed his locker shut.

"I have some stuff I need to do," he said evasively. Only Cami and his teachers knew Max went to tutoring two afternoons a week and Max aimed to keep it that way.

He slung his backpack over his shoulder and began walking down the hall with the three girls.

"See you later, then," Liz said as the three of them headed out into the icy afternoon.

"See you," Max said. The girls were hugging their coats tight and hurrying down the sidewalk but Max took his time walking into town. He loved Pine River winters — he found them refreshing, like pouring a cooler of ice water over his head after flag football practice.

Plus Max, like everyone else in town, loved Christmas and the lead-up to it. Every Wednesday through Saturday night in December, town officials brought cocoa and hot cider to Dobb's Hill, where there was midnight sledding (it ended at nine but "nine o'clock sledding" didn't sound as cool, Max figured). And there was a Christmas tradition of lighting a candle and placing it in the window as soon as the sun went down. Thinking of that now made Max's stomach turn. The candle would not be the same in the grimy window of the crummy rental apartment his family was living in now.

"Max, how are you?"

Max turned and saw Alma Sanchez, her curly gray hair falling out of a red felt hat. Max's mom had been one of the nurses who had cared for Ms. Sanchez's husband in the last few weeks of his life. After he died, Ms. Sanchez had thrown a huge dinner party to thank all of the healthcare providers who had helped make her husband's last days as comfortable as possible. There had been a lot of teary toasts, which had made Max squirm, but the food had been great and he knew Ms. Sanchez's appreciation had meant a lot to his mom.

"I'm okay, thanks," he said.

She rested a leather-gloved hand on one of his cheeks. "Your family has been through a lot," she said, her eyes full of sympathy. "Please let me know if there's anything at all I can do to help."

"Thanks," Max said. He could tell she really meant it, but it wasn't like he could ask her for what his family really needed. "We're okay."

"And keep warm in this weather," Ms. Sanchez added, pulling her coat tight as she walked down the street.

Max turned on Montgomery Street, then climbed up to the second story of the big brick building in the center of the block and knocked on Zoe's door. She opened it a moment later and ushered him in. Colored lights twinkled from the ceiling and the mantel over the crackling fire was covered with fresh pine branches, a bright red ribbon in the middle. Her tree stood in front of the big bay window, sparkling with tinsel and gold and silver balls. Zoe went for simple and elegant with her tree, unlike Max's family who had made new ornaments every year so that last year's tree was practically buried under a covering of felt angels, sequined balls, and paper rings. This year his mom and Fiona had baked play dough candy canes, nutcrackers, and angels that the whole family had painted. But they never had a chance to hang them because they, along with the rest of the ornaments, were gone, destroyed in the fire. The tree crammed into the corner of their rental was nearly bare, covered only with lights and colored balls a neighbor had given them. Max did all he could to avoid even looking at it and he suspected that his parents and sister did the same.

"How's it going?" Zoe asked Max, bringing him back into her cheery living room.

"All good," Max said. He walked over to the table in the corner that had three thick Christmas candles on it and began unpacking his school books. Zoe had been his tutor since second grade and this was the one place where he didn't have to come up with crazy pranks or witty remarks. Here he could just talk quietly with Zoe, get his work done, and enjoy feeling like a regular, normal kid.

And as he began to tell Zoe about his day, leaving out the visit to Ms. Sato's office, he realized what a relief that was.

Chapter 9

✦

Sixteen Days
until Christmas

Tuesday morning, like she had every day before they got Valentine, Lucy's mom walked her to school, depositing her in the lobby where Anya was waiting. It was utterly mortifying to be in sixth grade and dropped off by her mom, but there was no getting around it, not until Valentine healed.

But Valentine *would* heal and that mattered more than anything. The vet had called Saturday morning to say that the surgery had been a complete success. Valentine was cancer-free and once her body had recovered from the operation, she would be good as new. She had come home yesterday afternoon, tired but cheerful, trotting into the kitchen for dinner and snuggling down with Lucy in bed that night. She would be able to come back to school after a week of rest, and knowing that made everything else tolerable.

The hallway of Pine River Middle School was packed. Lucy could hear the footsteps of all the kids, heavy in winter boots. She heard their laughter and the little sighs of those who had not completed homework for their first class of the day. She felt the heat radiating off the boys who ran down the hall and the girls who pretended not to be following in their wake, their arms and backpacks brushing against Lucy as they passed. And of course there were the smells: syrup from morning waffles, wooly sweaters, damp mittens, strawberry shampoo, freshly applied lip gloss, and a thousand others that blended together into a potpourri that was fully and uniquely Pine River Middle School.

"Bye, Sweetness," her mom said, sneaking a surprise kiss onto Lucy's forehead. Lucy groaned and linked arms with Anya, who smelled like violet soap and peppermint toothpaste.

"I feel like I'm back in first grade," Lucy said as they started off down the hall, her walking stick clicking in front of her. Despite the stick and Anya's arm, she felt vulnerable, like she might accidently walk into an open locker or fall down a flight of stairs. It was only with Valentine that she felt safe walking down the crowded halls of the school.

"Don't worry about it," Anya said as they turned the corner. "No one even noticed."

Of course they had but it was nice of her friend to say that.

A group of boys yelling and smelling of sports socks and sweat ran by. Lucy cringed a little as one of them bumped into her.

"Sorry," he called as he sped past.

"Jerk," Anya muttered, pulling Lucy in closer to her. "How's Valentine?"

Lucy felt her shoulders, which had clenched up, relax at the thought of her dog. "She's great," she said. "Dr. Lazarus said the surgery went even better than she had hoped, and it was barely invasive so the recovery will be quick."

"And the prognosis is good?" Anya asked, stopping as they reached their lockers.

"It's terrific," Lucy said, a smile blooming across her face. "Valentine's going to be fine." She felt around the front pocket of her backpack for the lanyard with her locker key.

"That's so great," Anya said. Lucy could hear her rustling about in the papers that always covered the bottom of her locker.

"Yeah, it's huge," Lucy said. "I really thought I was going to lose her but thanks to the Angel Tree I'm not."

"The tree is awesome," Anya said. "I'm going to put up a wish for a brother swap, to see if I can trade in Theo for a brother who doesn't mess with my stuff all the time."

Lucy laughed; four-year-old Theo was a total terror.

"I wish I knew who set it up and makes sure all the wishes are granted," Lucy said. "I want to thank them, you know?"

She heard someone stop behind them for a moment and caught a whiff of bubble-gum lip balm. A girl scouting out the jock boys down the hall, no doubt.

"Yeah, but that's not how the tree works," Anya said, her voice muffled. She was digging deep in her locker. "Whoever is behind it doesn't want to be found out. They like the mystery of it."

It was hard to imagine someone not wanting to take credit for the fabulousness of the Angel Tree. It nagged at Lucy not to be able to do anything in return but she knew Anya was right. And really, what could she do anyway?

"Ready?" Anya asked, slamming her locker shut.

Lucy linked arms with her friend, set down the tip of her walking stick, and headed down the hall to homeroom.

When the bell for lunch rang, Anya guided Lucy to her locker before running off to her Robotics meeting. Lucy assured Anya that it was fine — and it was — but it still made her kind of anxious to navigate the halls with just her walking stick.

As Lucy popped open her locker, she could hear the crowd thinning out, a few girls talking as they walked by, and then a lone set of footsteps that stopped next to her. Lucy recognized the smell of the bubble-gum lip gloss from the morning.

"Hi, Lucy," a familiar voice said. "I'm Cami. We have language arts together."

They did, though Cami didn't speak all that much in class. The real reason Lucy remembered Cami was her violin playing at school assemblies and last year's Christmas Gala. Cami had made the instrument sing and her playing gave Lucy shivers of joy.

"Hi," Lucy said, carefully closing her locker. She figured Cami had stopped to see if she needed help and Lucy planned to politely turn her down. She was going to make this walk on her own.

"So, um, I heard you," Cami said. "Talking about the Angel Tree and how it helped your dog."

"Yeah," Lucy said, unsure why this was of interest to Cami.

"I have this idea," Cami said. Lucy could hear her shifting from one foot to the other and realized that Cami was nervous. "And Max is into it too. We want to find out who's behind the Angel Tree and give them the biggest, best thank-you ever."

"Oh, wow," Lucy said. "That sounds like a great idea."

"I'm glad you think so because I was hoping you might want to help us, you know, with finding out who's behind it and then planning a big surprise celebration to say thank you."

Lucy didn't know what to say. Right now she could barely walk down a hall on her own. How was she supposed to help uncover the secret angel behind the tree and then run around town planning a big thank-you party? Even with Valentine it was more than Lucy could imagine, way more than she had ever done on her own.

Camilla seemed to mistake her silence for disapproval. "I mean, I know the person behind it is supposed to be a mystery," she said hurriedly. "But he or she has been doing it for over twenty-five years. Don't you think it's time they got something in return, some kind of celebration to show how grateful we all are?"

Lucy definitely agreed but now another thought was occurring to her. Cami had to have other friends, friends who could see and be a hundred times more helpful than Lucy. So why was Cami here, asking her for help?

"Yeah, maybe you're right," Lucy said. "I'm just not sure how much I can help you. I mean, obviously I can't see anything and I don't get around easily. Don't you have other people you could ask, people more helpful than me?"

Cami coughed uncomfortably. "Well, actually right now I'm taking a bit of a break from my friends because pretty much all them except for Max are in the orchestra and I'm not —" She paused. "I'm just not hanging out with them right now. And anyway, the fact that you want to thank the person behind the tree — that matters way more than being able to see."

"I'm not so sure about that," Lucy said.

Cami laughed easily. "Believe me, if you want to help we can find all kinds of ways you can be part of it. That will be easy."

Lucy had to think Cami was mistaken. She had no idea of all the challenges that faced Lucy in a day.

"Please say yes," Cami said, laying her hand on Lucy's arm. "I know you want to."

She did, she really did. And so, despite all the reasons not to, Lucy agreed to meet up with Cami and Max after school the next day to begin coming up with a plan.

Dinner was ready by the time Anya had walked Lucy home and Lucy was famished. The smell of vegetable curry made her mouth water as she pulled off her snowy boots and Valentine came to greet her. Lucy was used to spending the whole day with her dog, so she took a minute to hug her tight. She'd missed her today. Valentine panted happily and licked Lucy's cheek.

"I'm happy to see you too, girl," Lucy told her.

Valentine thumped her tail on the wood floor, clearly feeling the same way.

Lucy heard her mom's footsteps padding in. "How was your day?" she asked.

"Good," Lucy said, her voice slightly muffled by Valentine's fur. She lifted up her head so that her mom could hear her. "How was yours?"

"Busy," her mom said, and Lucy could hear the tension in her voice. "But I did find the time to go by the drugstore. Mr. VonWolf already placed the order for Valentine's next round of meds and he said it's been covered by the Angel Tree, so that was helpful."

"Great," Lucy said, another wave of gratitude for the Angel Tree flowing over her. "How's Valentine?"

"I took her to Dr. Lazarus today," her mom said. "And she's very pleased with Valentine's progress. She should be able to take short trips by the weekend and ready for school on Monday."

"Great," Lucy said, bending over to give Valentine another hug. "Are you getting better?" she cooed. Valentine answered with another kiss on the cheek, this one extra slobbery, which made Lucy laugh.

"Your dad's on the phone but I think he'll be off soon and we can eat," her mom said, heading back toward the kitchen. "Dinner's ready."

At the sound of the word *dinner*, Valentine trotted for the kitchen, toenails clicking on the wood floor. "Okay, girl, it's dinner time for you too," Lucy said as she followed behind. She got out a can of food and attached it carefully to the can opener while Valentine whined eagerly. Lucy removed the lid with a fork the way her mom had taught her, then scraped the food into Valentine's dish. She was rewarded with the snuffling sounds of Valentine inhaling her meal.

Lucy slid on her fleece slippers and returned to the dining room.

A minute later Lucy heard her dad's steps, not his old-man shuffle but steps that were quick and light. She hoped this meant that his phone call was good, or at least not another bill collector or membership that had to be canceled.

Once they were all around the table Lucy's dad served her. "Curry's at one o'clock, rice is at six," he said. "And I put a bit of that mint chutney you like over at nine."

"Thanks," Lucy said, picking up her fork. It was much easier to eat when she knew where everything was on her plate, which she treated as the face of a clock. A moment later she felt a wet nose on her ankle. Valentine always tried to sneak in when they were eating, hoping for some scraps from the table. Usually her parents shooed the dog out but tonight they didn't notice she was there.

"I just had a very interesting call from Kira Cutler," her dad said.

Lucy recognized the name of one of the local architects her dad sometimes worked with and she paused, fork in midair, to hear what Ms. Cutler wanted.

"It turns out she's part of a big building project that started out as a wish on the Angel Tree," her dad went on. "She asked if I'd be willing to volunteer my time to help out. It's going to be a community undertaking, with a whole group of folks pitching in."

"That's wonderful," Lucy's mom said. "And it's great they asked you to help out."

"It is," her dad said, his fork scraping along his plate as he scooped up a bite of curry. "It'll be good to have somewhere to go every day. And to be part of something meaningful."

"Absolutely," her mom said.

"Do you know what kind of building it is?" Lucy asked.

"She didn't say," her dad said. "But I'm up for anything."

It was terrific to hear her dad sound so excited about something, and it reminded Lucy of her talk with Cami. "Dad," she asked. "Did Ms. Cutler say anything about the person behind the Angel Tree?"

"I asked who was organizing the building project, actually," her dad said. "Because it's an awfully big thing to pull together. But even Kira has no idea who's behind it. Everything is communicated through a general email and no one has any idea who's pulling the strings. It's very Bond-worthy actually." Her dad loved James Bond, so this was a true compliment. Though unfortunately it did not help Lucy at all.

Still, it was something to tell the others when they met the next day, and even though she was feeling worried that her presence wouldn't help, she had to admit she was looking forward to the meeting.

Chapter 10

✳

Fifteen Days
until Christmas

The halls were crowded as Cami made her way to her locker after school on Wednesday. She'd taken the long way to avoid passing the orchestra room, which still made her throat tighten every time she walked by. Her arms felt oddly empty without her violin case, and keeping distance from her music friends to duck their questions about her missing rehearsals was getting harder and harder. All of which had made Cami decide that she needed a second project.

Joe was stuffing books in his backpack when Cami finally made it, his cheeks a healthy pink, the corners of his mouth turned up just slightly. On Monday when he had first gotten whatever news that made him so happy,

Cami had heard him whisper the words *Angel Tree*. Which totally made sense. What else would bring such happiness to someone as sad as Joe?

And that was why Cami had come to the decision to make Joe her other project. Reaching out to an isolated student was just the sort of thing Willa would do and it would make a very nice story at dinner for her grandmother. And right now she needed as many nice stories as she could get, because so far her attempts to help had fallen short or gone totally unnoticed. So even though Max was going to fight her on it, Cami's new mission was to convince him to let Joe join them in her bigger quest, the one to find the person behind the Angel Tree. And the time to do that was now.

Cami gave Joe a big smile, grabbed her stuff out of her locker, and hurried to meet Lucy and Max before Joe left the building. Cami had noticed he often lingered after the last bell, so she figured she had about ten minutes to talk Max into her plan.

"Hi, Cami," Lucy said when Cami was still more than ten feet away.

"Hi," Cami said as she came closer. "How did you know it was me?"

Lucy's face, which was a frown of concentration as she put her books into her bag, slipped into a brief grin. "Your bubble-gum lip gloss," she said.

Cami was impressed. "Really? You can smell it that far away?"

Lucy nodded, twining a beautiful maroon scarf around her neck. "Blind people's other senses get really good, to compensate for not being able to see, I guess."

"That seems like a good thing," Cami said.

Lucy wrinkled her nose. "Not in the cafeteria," she said, and Cami laughed, thinking of yesterday's meatloaf special that was anything but special.

"Hello, ladies," called Ms. Marwich. She was walking down the hall, looking calm despite the chaos of running and yelling kids all around her.

"Hi," Cami said, smiling like she always did when she saw the friendly librarian. Her hair was falling out of its bun and her comfortable old sweater had a few bits of cat hair clinging to it. Ms. Marwich kept a picture of her cat, Tango, on her desk and sometimes entertained students with stories of his adventures chasing mice in the backyard.

"What does Ms. Marwich smell like?" Cami asked Lucy after she'd passed.

"She wears a rose lotion," Lucy said, but then her brow creased slightly. "And she smelled like something else today too. Lavender, I think."

Max was walking toward them, his backpack half open and a hat falling out of his coat pocket. "Let's go talk at Cinnamon's," he said. "I'm dying for one of their doughnuts."

"Sounds good," Cami said, and took a deep breath. "And I had an idea. I think we should ask Joe to come too. I want him to help us find out who's behind the Angel Tree."

At that, Max's whole body went stiff. "What?" he asked.

"I just — Max, he looks so lonely all the time," Cami pleaded. "And the other day I think he got a wish granted because it was the first time all year I saw him smile and he said the words *Angel Tree* so I think he'd —"

"No way," Max said firmly.

"Sometimes people have a story," Cami said, thinking of her violin and how her music friends probably thought she was being a jerk when in fact she'd do almost anything to be back practicing with them.

"That's a good point," Lucy said thoughtfully.

They both turned to her.

"I mean, we all have reasons why we do things," Lucy went on. "And they're not always obvious."

"He didn't have a good reason for punching me," Max said, though Cami could tell he found it harder to argue with Lucy than he did with her.

"Lucy's right," Cami said, jumping on that. "Let's give him a chance."

"It would be the Christmassy thing to do," Lucy added.

"He'll say no," Max said. "He's not going to want to do anything with me."

"So then we just ask," Cami said, feeling that victory was close. "And if he says no, that's the end of it."

Max shrugged. "Whatever," he said, but his easy smile was gone.

"Thanks," Cami said gratefully. Then she headed down the hall. "I'm going to see if I can catch him at his locker. I'll meet you guys at the front door in five minutes!"

"I love how it smells in here," Cami said to Lucy and Max as she pushed open the door of Cinnamon Bakery, the warm air swirling around them, thick with chocolate, butter, and, of course, cinnamon.

Max just shrugged, his face sullen. Joe had agreed to meet them after he finished a project in the computer room and Max did not seem happy about it.

"Yeah, it's pretty heavenly," Lucy agreed as Cami led her over to a table by the window.

Max followed, his steps exaggeratedly heavy, like he was walking to an execution. Cami tried not to roll her eyes. She got that Max didn't like Joe but it was time to put their fight in the past and move on. They had bigger things to worry about now.

The wooden tables and chairs of Cinnamon Bakery were painted a cherry red that stood out against the snowy white walls. Black-and-white photos of the original Cinnamon, a fat dachshund, dotted the walls. She was the childhood pet of Syda and Clementine Wilson, the sisters who owned the bakery. Like all the other stores in town, Cinnamon's was decked out for Christmas.

A Christmas tree stood in the corner decorated with ornaments in the shape of baked goods, its lights blinking on and off. Matching lights were strung around the ceiling and small ceramic angels sat on the windowsill and next to the cash register on the counter.

"Hey, guys, what can I get for you today? Cinnamon doughnuts?" Syda asked as she walked over to their table, her long hair held back with rhinestone clips. The sisters did everything from baking to mopping up at night and knew pretty much everyone in town by name and favorite baked good.

"Perfect," Cami said. "We'll take a dozen." She glanced out the big glass windows. Through the steam from the ovens in back she could see Joe coming down the sidewalk, hands jammed into his pockets, his head down.

"Joe's coming," she announced as he pulled open the door. Lucy smiled but Max's mouth pulled tight, as though he had just eaten a bad piece of sausage.

"Hey," Joe said, sliding into the seat across from Lucy. He hunched down a bit, clearly trying to warm up from the chilly walk. Cami didn't understand why Joe didn't have better winter clothes but she certainly wasn't going to ask. It did not take a genius to guess how that conversation would go.

"We ordered doughnuts," Cami said.

"And here they are," Syda said, coming up and setting a heaping platter of fluffy cinnamon-and-sugar-coated twists on the table. She looked closely at Joe. "I don't think we've met. I'm Syda, one of the owners of this crazy place." She stuck out her hand and, after hesitating for a moment, Joe reached out and shook it.

"Joe," he said. "Nice to meet you."

"Are you visiting?" Syda asked, setting a small plate in front of each of them.

Joe shook his head, frowning slightly. "No," he said.

They all waited but he didn't offer more.

Feeling awkward, Cami jumped in. "Joe moved here at the beginning of the school year," she said. She was about to say where he'd come from but then realized she had no idea.

"Well, welcome, Joe," Syda said gently. "I hope to see you again soon."

"Um, thanks," Joe said as she walked away.

"Let's get started," Cami said as everyone dug into the doughnuts. They looked scrumptious but she didn't want to risk having her mouth full if the guys started fighting, so she waited to take one. "How are we going to find the Great Benefactor?"

Max's eyebrows scrunched up. "The what?"

"Well, Head Honcho Angel isn't right. And Santa's Angel just sounds dumb. So: the Great Benefactor," Cami repeated. "I think that's what we should call the person behind the Angel Tree."

Max was nodding. "A code name," he said. "I like that. But it should just be the initials. GB."

Cami couldn't help grinning. She'd come up with the name for Max, knowing his obsession with anything spy related. And sure enough he was looking more cheerful as he reached for his third doughnut.

"So what's our plan to find the — GB?" Cami asked.

"I had an idea," Max said. "In the movies they sometimes make a profile of the person they're searching for, like a list of traits that serial killers have or whatever. It helps narrow down the search."

"So we should make a list of traits that serial *givers* have?" Cami asked, laughing.

"Something like that," Max said. Cami could tell he was getting excited about the plan when he didn't even pause to acknowledge her joke. She began to relax just the littlest bit. "Like one obvious trait is that GB probably has money. I mean, you'd have to be rich to be able to get the tree and take care of all the leftover wishes."

Things were going well, so Cami risked picking up her doughnut and biting through the crisp outer layer to the fluffy insides, the sugar and cinnamon melting on her tongue.

Lucy was nodding as she wiped some sugar off her chin. "That's smart," she said. "Also, GB is probably really into Pine River. What's the town equivalent of school spirit?"

"Town spirit," Cami said, smiling.

Max laughed. "Totally. And I was thinking that GB might not have a full-time job or young kids. Because organizing the Angel Tree and all the wishes would take tons of time."

"That's a good point," Cami said.

"Not necessarily." Joe spoke up for the first time. "It might just be someone who's incredibly dedicated to something they believe in and who finds the time to make it happen."

"In a profile you're just going for the most likely scenario," Max said irritably. "And GB not working is the more likely situation."

Joe looked like he was about to argue, so Cami dropped her doughnut back on her plate and spoke up quickly. "Okay, this is a great profile," she said. "Who do we think fits it?"

"I have some ideas about that too," Max said, glaring at Joe.

"Who?" Lucy asked.

"I think our first suspect is —" Max beat a drumroll on the table. "Mr. Pink!" Max looked around the table proudly. "It's obvious, really. He has money and a lot of workers in his store —"

"The Handyman Hardware Store, on Main Street," Cami broke in, realizing Joe probably didn't know who Mr. Pink was. "And by the way, you can't call possible GBs *suspects*. They didn't commit a crime."

"— so Mr. Pink would have the time," Max continued, ignoring Cami's remark. "He definitely has town spirit. And he's generous, always giving people discounts when they don't have enough money to buy the things they need."

"That's true," Cami said. "Mr. Pink is worth checking out." She thought back to the time Mr. Pink had announced a one-day sale on screwdrivers when her grandmother had been short a dollar on the one they needed. Then someone else occurred to her, someone just as generous as Mr. Pink. "I have another name to add. I think we should check out the VonWolfs." Cami looked around eagerly to see how the others reacted to her idea. "They fit the profile: They're always helping at town festivals, and they live in a huge mansion."

"They own the drugstore, right?" Joe asked.

"Yeah, but they're mostly retired," Cami said. "So they have time."

Max was nodding. "Good call. We'll definitely check them out."

Cami's cheeks felt warm with pleasure at the compliment as she reached for another doughnut.

"I think we should add Alma Sanchez," Lucy said. "Her husband left her a lot of money when he died. Plus she organizes a lot of events around town like the Christmas Gala."

"She should definitely be on the list," Max agreed.

Lucy was feeling her watch, which had really cool Braille dots and hands that Lucy could touch. "You guys, I have to go in a minute," she said. "We're actually going to get our Christmas tree today."

"Sounds fun," Cami said happily. The meeting had been a huge success and she was certain they'd find GB in no time. She waved at Syda and asked for the check, then pulled out her phone so she could keep track of their list. "Okay, we have Mr. Pink, the VonWolfs, Alma Sanchez. Anyone else?" she asked as she typed in their names.

"At first I was thinking of Dr. Lazarus," Lucy said. "But she doesn't totally fit the profile. She's super busy, and I don't think she actually lives in Pine River."

Cami hesitated, then nodded. "Okay, let's leave her off. I think we should stick with people who fit our profile, at least for now."

Lucy nodded.

"I have one more I think we should add," Max said. "What about the Barristers?"

Cami frowned. "I don't really see that," she said.

Lucy shook her head slightly. "That is *really* hard to imagine."

"But that's why it's total genius," Max said, his eyes bright. He was clearly still in spy mode. "You'd never guess them, which is the perfect cover."

"Who are the Barristers?" Joe asked, looking at Cami.

"This weird old couple —" Max started.

"They're not that weird," Cami said. "They just, uh, hardly ever come out of their house and when they do they never talk to anyone."

"There are all kinds of stories about them," Max continued. "Like that they work for the CIA. Or are political fugitives. No one knows for sure, but they've got to have some kind of secret, and that's why they stay hidden all the time."

"But you still think they might be GB?" Cami asked. She wasn't buying it.

Max nodded. "Just think about it," he said grandly, clearly loving his theory. "This whole time they act like they're not part of the town but secretly they're the force behind the town's most famous tradition."

Cami could tell Max was doing his typical Max thing, getting totally carried away, but Lucy was nodding. "Max could be right," she said.

Max grinned at Cami, who rolled her eyes. It seemed like a waste of time but if it made him happy, it was fine by her. "Is there anyone else?"

"I don't really know anyone in town," Joe said. "But I was thinking about another trait we should add to the profile."

Cami looked at him, surprised and pleased he wanted to contribute something. Once he was really part of things, she could casually mention to her grandmother how she had helped bring him out of his shell. "That's great! What?" she asked, trying to sound extra supportive.

"It's probably someone who doesn't have a big ego," Joe said. "I mean, they do all this awesome stuff but never want credit for it. I don't know many people like that." He shot a pointed look at Max.

Cami hoped that Max didn't see it but his face immediately darkened. "What's that supposed to mean?" he snapped.

"Just that someone like you would never do something like that," Joe muttered with venom. This was *not* what Cami hoped would happen when he came out of his shell.

"You don't know anything about me," Max said hotly.

Cami saw that he was squeezing his hands into fists, and she jumped in, desperate to stop this before it got bad. "Knock it off you guys. We don't have time for this. There're only fifteen days till Christmas, when we have to know who GB is and have a whole party planned. So let's just finish our list."

But Max was pushing back his chair so hard it hit the wall behind him with a thud. "I don't need this," he said. "I'm done helping you guys if he's going to be hanging around." He stomped to the door and headed out into the cold.

"Sorry," Joe said, not sounding sorry at all.

Now that she saw how much he truly disliked Max, Cami did not understand why Joe had ever agreed to help them. But there was no way he was getting out of it now.

"It's not all right," Cami snapped. "And we're still meeting Friday after school to start our investigation."

"I think we should go to Pine Forest," Lucy said.

Cami was grateful for Lucy's optimism in the face of the disaster that had just happened.

"Pine Forest is the Christmas Tree farm where almost everyone gets their trees," Cami explained to Joe. "If GB got the Angel Tree from Pine Forest, it might be a good place to start looking for clues."

"I'll be there," Joe said. "But I can't speak for anyone else." He seemed cheerful as he put on his coat and headed out.

"That didn't go well," Cami said with a sigh. There was no way she could tell her grandmother about the meeting now.

"Well, maybe Max will change his mind," Lucy said, clearly not believing a word of it.

Cami had the sneaking suspicion that her great plan was over before it could start.

"Here's your check," Syda said, setting it down. "And aren't you ladies generous to treat."

Cami would have laughed if she'd had it in her. Of course the boys had stuck her and Lucy with the bill. The not-so-perfect ending to a not-so-perfect afternoon.

Chapter 11

Fifteen Days
until Christmas

Max hated Joe. Hated him. The guy was a menace. If they hadn't been in Cinnamon's with half the town around, Max would have . . .

But he couldn't do that to his family, not now. The thing he could do, though, was stay as far away from Joe as possible. That would mean missing out on finding GB but at this point Max didn't care. The only reason he had agreed to help was that it sounded fun to track down the mysterious person behind the tree, kind of like being a spy. Now, though, it was anything but fun. So he was out and that was the end of it. He was annoyed with Cami for asking Joe in the first place and he honestly had no idea why Joe had agreed, seeing how much he obviously despised Max.

Stalking through the snow, Max had reached the corner of Main Street and Church and for a moment he glanced wistfully down Church, where the remains of his home stood. Then he sighed and headed down Montgomery toward the small apartment building next to Handyman Hardware.

As he came up to the building Max told himself that the apartment wasn't *that* bad. It was just small and dark with mold in the corners and a bathroom that reeked of mildew. . . . Okay, maybe it was that bad. Max didn't really know; all he knew was how much he hated living there and how much he missed his home.

He pulled open the heavy glass door and was surprised to see Mr. Pink bent over and squinting at the lobby mailboxes, his bald head shiny under the sharp fluorescent lights.

"Max, just the person I'm looking for," Mr. Pink said, straightening up.

For a moment Max wondered if Mr. Pink had been eavesdropping at the bakery. "Really?" he asked, baffled that Mr. Pink wanted to talk to him.

Mr. Pink laughed and Max realized his response was less then polite. Good thing his mom hadn't overheard — she was big with manners.

"Yes, indeed," Mr. Pink said, straightening and rubbing his hands together. "I need a favor and you're the one who can make it happen."

"Okay," Max said, confused as to how he could possibly help Mr. Pink.

"Do you think you could get your family to come to the Angel Tree tomorrow night at seven?" Mr. Pink asked.

"Why?" Max asked. He knew it wasn't the polite response but he was too curious to worry about it.

"Good, I've piqued your interest," Mr. Pink said, pulling a wool hat out of the pocket of his down jacket. "I assume that means your answer is a yes?" He put the hat on and moved toward the door.

"Yes," Max said.

Mr. Pink gave him a thumbs-up and headed out into the night, leaving Max staring after him and hoping against hope that the appointment would have something to do with his wish.

Chapter 12

✳

Fifteen Days
until Christmas

The frosty night bit into Joe as he walked home
from Cinnamon's, the sweet taste of sugar still
on his tongue. He hugged his thin jacket around
his shoulders, thinking about the afternoon and wondering if he had really made the right choice to help find GB.

If it had been the week before, Joe would have turned
Cami down flat the second she revealed that Max was in
on the project. But when his wish was granted, things
changed. Or more accurately, they were going to have
to change. Because Joe had spent the last five months
lying to his mom and now that she was really and truly
coming to Pine River, Joe was going to have to twist
some of those lies into the truth.

Although Joe liked to remember the good things about his life in Virginia — his mom making peanut brittle for their weekly movie nights, friends coming over after soccer, walks through the woods outside town — certain things had been hard and they all boiled down to one thing: money. After his dad had taken off, leaving them in terrible debt, his mom simply couldn't make enough to cover their bills. They cut corners, patching old clothes instead of getting new ones and walking to avoid having to put gas in the car. But first the electricity was cut, then the gas, and then they were on the verge of being kicked out of their home.

That was when Joe's mom sat down and explained that she needed to make a hard decision: It would be tough on both of them but she was going to enlist in the marines. Money would be tight for the next few years as they paid off their debt and she served, but the work she was doing was important, worth the sacrifice. There were other things she might have done to make money, but this was the one she believed in: fighting for the country she loved. And in the end it would help them both.

Joe had readily agreed. He accepted leaving every-thing he loved to live with Uncle Leon and going to a strange school where everyone hated him. He learned to block out his fears that his mother would be harmed in the line of duty. And he had even accepted that there was no way to spend Christmas with his mother, that despite her five-day leave to the base in Florida they could not afford a plane ticket to northern Pennsylvania. But now, thanks to the Angel Tree, they could.

Which was amazing but also a problem.

"Do you want to come over for dinner?"

Joe looked up but of course the boy was talking to his friend, not Joe. Joe was passing Dobb's Hill, where a bunch of kids were out sledding, shrieking as they flew down the icy hill, then milling around at the bottom, talking and making plans to hang out together.

"Yeah, let me just call my mom," the other boy answered.

No one noticed as Joe passed by, a slight shadow under the glowing streetlights.

And this, of course, was Joe's problem. His mom believed that Joe loved Pine River, that he had friends over all the time and that he'd never been happier. She believed these things because that's what Joe had told her. If she knew the truth, she would be concerned about him and that wouldn't be right. Joe told her stories of his good friends and good times in Pine River to make her happy, so she could focus on staying alive and not worry about her son back home.

Until now when she was actually coming to Pine River and would see that not only was Joe friendless, he was hated. So when Cami asked if he would help out with finding GB, Joe had jumped at the chance to do something he could tell his mom about, something that involved other people. Sure, he was happy to thank GB, who had given him the best gift ever. But he'd never have agreed to a plan involving Max if it wasn't for his mom.

Joe had reached the run-down building that housed a Laundromat on the first floor and two small apartments above. He looked up and saw that the windows in Leon's apartment were dark. Joe never knew how to talk to Leon, who usually came home late and mostly pretended Joe wasn't there, so this was a relief.

But as Joe climbed the narrow, rickety stairs, there was a hollow feeling in his chest that came from one too many dinners alone. This emptiness that was Joe's whole life was exactly what his mom could never see. And so, as he turned the key in the lock and opened the door to the smell of old socks and burnt burgers, Joe vowed to keep meeting Cami and Lucy, and do whatever he could to stay connected to something in Pine River, something that would make his mother happy.

Chapter 13

Fourteen Days
until Christmas

It was a lot harder to convince his family that they needed to go the Angel Tree than Max had thought it would be. Fiona had a cold, his dad was exhausted from a double shift at the post office, and his mom had planned a night of laundry and an early bedtime. None of them wanted to venture out in the polar night air, even though the tree was only half a block away.

"I promised Mr. Pink," Max pleaded, his eyes on the clock, which now read 6:46.

"I don't understand any of this," his mom said with a sigh. "But I suppose a promise is a promise."

"What could Mr. Pink want?" his dad wondered, slowly pulling on his winter jacket.

"He didn't say anything?" Max's mom asked as she stuffed a complaining Fiona into a fleece vest and the secondhand coat she'd picked up at the church thrift shop.

"No," Max said, opening the door to the apartment in hopes that it would encourage his parents to hurry. He had had his own coat on for the past ten minutes and was starting to sweat.

"All right, let's go," his mom said, her voice tired. Max saw the dark circles under her eyes. His mom always had insomnia when she was anxious about something and from the looks of things she hadn't slept in weeks.

His family made their way down the narrow stairs and out through the lobby.

"It's too cold," Fiona whined.

Max squelched the urge to give her a pinch.

The town square was deserted as Max's family made their way over to the Angel Tree. A light snow was falling, the icy kind that was more crystals than flakes. Max could feel them clinging to his eyelashes and brows.

"So what are we waiting for?" his dad asked.

And then they saw it, a line of people walking toward them led by Mr. Pink. At first the others were in the shadows of the street lamps that hung on each corner of the square but as they came closer Max recognized Ann and Jim Bellows, who ran a local contracting firm, along with the town electrician and plumber, and Kira Cutler, who owned an architecture firm. Max's heart was thumping hard in his chest as they came and stood before his family.

"Thanks for coming out tonight," Mr. Pink said to Max and his family. "And we won't keep you wondering about why we've dragged you out in the cold. Come the first day of spring, these people" — he gestured to the group gathered around him — "and a slew of helpers are going to start breaking ground on your new house."

Max's mother gasped and grabbed his father's arm, which wasn't a great idea because his father looked like he was about to faint.

"We wanted to gather here at the Angel Tree to tell you in person," Mr. Pink went on. "Because this tree symbolizes what our community is about and here, at this tree, the call for help is answered."

Max's father still looked stunned but his mom reached over and rested a hand on Max's back. "Did you put up a wish?" she asked softly.

Max nodded, his throat suddenly too thick to speak.

"I don't know if we can accept this," she said, turning back to Mr. Pink. "The insurance will only cover part of the expense and —"

Mr. Pink held up a hand. "We know," he said simply.

"But the cost, your time," Max's father said, looking around. "It's too much to ask of any of you."

"We give it willingly," Mr. Pink said, and the group around him, their faces bathed in the light from the Christmas lights strung on the buildings around them, nodded.

Max's father opened his mouth to speak again but his mom put her hand on his arm. "Thank you," she said, her voice hoarse. "Thank you so much for this incredible gift."

Mr. Pink grinned. "Merry Christmas," he said.

Fiona stepped forward looking up at Mr. Pink with wonder. "Are you Santa?" she asked.

Everyone laughed, including Max, but as he looked around at the people gathered there to help his family, he did feel like maybe Santa had just paid them an early visit. Then he glanced at the tree behind them, dark against the blue-black night sky, and knew that what had happened tonight was something even better because it was real. It was the Angel Tree that had brought together the people of Pine River to make his impossible wish come true.

Chapter 14

Thirteen Days until Christmas

S o I'll pick you up in an hour?" Lucy's mom asked as Lucy opened the door of their car on Friday after school, a frigid breeze slipping in from the parking lot of Pine Forest Christmas Trees.

"I think that's enough time," Lucy said, stepping out and then holding the door for Valentine, who hopped out next to her. "But I'm not sure."

"I don't mind waiting," her mom said. "We want to be careful not to tire Valentine."

"Right," Lucy agreed, leaning down to rub her dog's head. The vet had okayed an hour or two of activity for Valentine, and Lucy wanted to be sure to follow those orders carefully so that Valentine could continue to heal. "Thanks, Mom."

"Happy to do it," her mom said. "It's about ten steps to the front gate but it looks like your friend is coming to get you."

"See you later," Lucy said, closing the car door and following as Valentine began leading her to the gate.

"Hey, Lucy," Cami said, her boots crunching in the snow.

"Hi," Lucy said. She heard a rustling sound, most likely Cami waving to her mom as she drove away.

"So we'll wait for Joe and then — oh, wow!"

Lucy was about to ask what had Cami so excited when she smelled clean gym socks, fried eggs, and hot cocoa, and heard Max's laugh.

"Surprised?" he asked as he came up to them.

"I can't believe you're here!" Cami exclaimed joyfully.

"Yeah, well, my Angel Tree wish came true so I figured I owed it to GB to be part of your big thank-you celebration," Max said. Max always sounded cheerful but today his voice was positively exuberant.

"What wish?" Cami asked.

"Oh, no big deal, just a whole new house," Max said. He was making light of it, but Lucy could hear that he was bouncing on his toes as he spoke.

Cami squealed in delight and Lucy heard the soft sounds of her hugging Max.

"Oh," Lucy exclaimed, suddenly remembering her dad's new volunteer job. "I think my dad is going to be helping out!"

"Awesome," Max said. "Tell him I said thanks."

"That's so cool," Cami said, giving her arm a squeeze.

"And here's someone that's totally *not* cool," Max muttered.

Lucy did not need to smell the approaching mix of laundry soap and lemon cleaner to know that Joe had arrived.

"So we're all here," Cami said cheerfully. "Let's go!"

Lucy followed as they walked through the gate of Pine Forest. People around them were laughing and there was the feathery sound of families loading up Christmas trees to take home. Lucy had been coming here with her parents for years so she knew that just inside was the fenced-off area where precut trees were stacked. There was a small wooden cabin, where people could buy hot cider or wreathes when they paid for their trees, or just warm up before venturing out to the acres beyond, which were thick with growing pine trees of every shape and size.

"So where should we start looking?" Max asked.

"We should ask the owner if he knows anything about GB," Joe said.

"If Mr. Saint-Pierre knows anything, he won't say," Max said coolly. Lucy could feel Cami tense next to her.

"But maybe he'll say something that gives us a clue," Joe persisted.

"That's a great idea," Cami said quickly.

Max sighed but he didn't put up a fight.

Lucy heard Mr. Saint-Pierre's fingers tapping on the old-fashioned cash register as they walked into the heat of the little cabin that smelled of cinnamon-laced cider. Lucy took advantage of the moment to rest Valentine, who was panting slightly. Joe's sneakers padded closer to the wood stove while Cami stayed next to Lucy, and Max wandered around, unable to keep still.

"How can I help you kids?" Mr. Saint-Pierre asked in his low voice a few moments later. Lucy's parents had described his wild mustache and flowing beard that had half the kids under six thinking he was Santa Claus, a role he often played at the town Christmas Gala.

Lucy hesitated, wondering how to explain their mission, but Cami spoke up right away. "We're hoping to find out some information about the person behind the Angel Tree," she said, getting right to it.

"I'm sorry, kids, but I can't help you with that," Mr. Saint-Pierre said.

"We know it's supposed to be a secret," Cami said. "But this is important. We want to do something to thank the person who's been working so hard for all these years."

"I wish I could help, I truly do," he said. "But I have no idea who does it. Every year I get a hand-delivered letter that there's going to be a pickup for a tree that's already been selected. They must come in the middle of the night to choose the tree, mark it with a ribbon, and then pay a trucker to come get it and put it up in town. And I bet the trucker knows even less than I do. We're both paid in cash and that's the end of it. Every year, that's how it goes."

"Do you still have the letter?" Lucy asked.

"No, it went out with the recycling weeks ago," Mr. Saint-Pierre said. A bell jingled as the door to the cabin opened and a family came in, two little kids running ahead and giggling. Lucy and Cami turned to go but then Joe spoke up.

"Can you tell us what section of the forest the tree was taken from this year?" he asked.

"Sure," Mr. Saint-Pierre said. "And to be honest I'm not sure anyone else has been back in that section. It's where we have our biggest trees and we usually just sell a handful of those every year."

"And you haven't sold any others yet?" Cami asked, excited.

"Nope," Mr. Saint-Pierre said. "Not yet." There was the crinkly sound of paper as he handed something to Cami. "Here's a map. The section you're interested in is all the way back here," he said. Lucy assumed he was pointing to a spot on the map. "So it doesn't get much traffic."

"This is great," Cami said. "Thanks so much, Mr. Saint-Pierre."

The others echoed their thanks and headed back out into the cold for the trek to the far section of the forest. Valentine seemed energetic and happy as she pranced carefully through the snow, leading Lucy on a wide, clear path through the rows and rows of balsam fir, Scotch pine, blue spruce, and white pine trees, each with a slightly different scent.

At first they followed paths made by trails of footprints, the snow packed down tight under Lucy's feet. But by the time they reached their destination, the snow was untouched and harder to navigate.

"No one's been here since last night's snow," Max said, his boots crunching on the crusty top layer, then breaking through with a crackle.

"That's good," Cami said. She had slowed down to stay next to Lucy and Valentine.

"Except that any clues GB left last week would probably be covered," Max said.

"Not necessarily," Joe said, clearly eager to disagree with Max.

"What do you know about it?" Max snapped. "Is there even snow where you come from?"

"Since we're here let's look around," Cami interrupted before things could get heated between Max and Joe. "Something might have gotten caught in one of the trees or something. Let's spread out and search."

Lucy gave Valentine's lead a light tug and the dog,

who had been resting, struggled to her feet. Lucy knew walking in the high snow was hard for Valentine and decided she would only cover a little ground. It wasn't like she was going to find a clue anyway. She gave Valentine a free lead and let the dog choose their direction and the pace.

They walked through evenly spaced trees on a low slope of land. The branches rustled around them, and farther off Lucy could hear Max and Cami talking and laughing.

But then Valentine tensed and picked up her pace. Clearly she had spotted something interesting, and Lucy hoped it wasn't a squirrel out searching for a snack. Valentine was extremely well trained and would never chase a squirrel, but she did like to look at them and yip.

It wasn't a squirrel that had caught the Lab's attention, though. It was something buried in the snow. Valentine burrowed her snout in, the ice crunching as she dug down, and a moment later she pulled something up, shaking off the snow with a musical clink of the dog tags on her collar.

"What is it, girl?" Lucy asked, holding out her gloved hand.

Valentine set the object carefully in Lucy's palm. Lucy took off her glove so she could feel what it was. It was covered with a thin sheen of ice, but as the warmth of Lucy's fingers melted that, it revealed a thick rectangle of leather, about two inches wide and eight inches long. Delighted with her find, she hurried back to the spot where the others were gathering.

"I didn't see anything," Cami was saying gloomily as Lucy and Valentine approached. "I guess it was —" She broke off as Lucy held up the leather strip.

"I found something," Lucy said. "Actually Valentine did. I guess she smelled it or something because she started digging through the snow and came up with this."

"What is it?" Cami asked as the three of them crowded around Lucy and Valentine.

"I'm not sure," Lucy said. "She had it in her mouth. Take a look and you tell me."

Cami reached over and took the small object from Lucy. Both Joe and Max leaned in for a closer look.

"I think it's a bookmark," Cami said after a moment. "It's swollen from the snow but you can see carvings in it, like ivy going up the sides."

"Do you think it belonged to GB?" Lucy asked.

"It seems like a safe bet, doesn't it?" Cami asked, her voice buoyant. "Guys, we have our first clue!"

"So what does it tell us?" Joe asked as they started back toward the parking lot and the road to town. His teeth were nearly chattering.

"That GB is a reader, obviously," Max said in a withering tone.

"Yeah, but it tells us even more than that," Cami said before Joe could respond. "I mean, a fancy bookmark like this tells us that GB really cares about books. Real books, too, not ebooks."

"That's probably a sign that GB's a little older," Lucy said, thinking that her parents read print books while her teenage cousins all read ebooks.

"Good point," Cami said.

"And also it could mean it's someone with a huge home library," Lucy said, slipping a little on an icy patch but righting herself quickly. "You would only get a nice bookmark if you had a lot of books to read."

They were back in the more populated section of the farm. There were voices around them and walking was easier now that there were footpaths to follow. Lucy could tell Valentine was tired and she took a moment to rub the dog's floppy ears. After all, Valentine had been the hero of the day, finding their very first clue.

"Let's meet up tomorrow for more investigating," Cami said. "The Angel Tree, ten o'clock."

The others agreed, but Valentine was panting again and Lucy knew she would need to let her dog rest the next day so that she would be ready for school on Monday. Lucy wasn't sure if it made sense for her to go along tomorrow without the dog for help. She was pretty sure she'd just drag everything down, with people needing to take care of her instead of looking for more clues. Plus she had plans to go over to Anya's in the afternoon. But as the others waited for her reply, Lucy changed her mind. Finding GB was important and Anya would understand. Plus Lucy had helped find the very first clue, which meant she was being helpful. She was probably worrying over nothing.

"I'll be there," she said.

Chapter 15

✳

Twelve Days until Christmas

The others were standing in front of the Angel Tree when Max arrived the next morning. He had overslept and barely had time to wolf down some toast before throwing on his jacket and heading for the meeting. Cami was chatting with Joe and Lucy but she broke off when she saw Max approach. Max braced himself for the inevitable scolding that he knew was coming: Cami did not tolerate lateness. But to his surprise, Cami just smiled sweetly and greeted him with great cheer.

Max was instantly suspicious. "What's going on?" he asked.

Cami's eyes widened and an ominous feeling began building in Max's gut. "Nothing, I'm just glad you're here," she said, her voice way too sugary. "Now we can get started."

Max decided not to press the issue but his guard was up. He greeted Lucy and then pointedly turned his back on Joe, who was shivering pathetically in his thin jacket. "So what's the plan?" he asked.

"Today we start investigating our possible suspects — I mean, GBs," Cami said.

"Excellent," Max said, rubbing his hands together. He was ready to go undercover.

"I was thinking we should come up with reasons to visit everyone on our list," Cami said. "Then we work the conversation around to the Angel Tree and look for clues, any change in expression, or a slipup where they know more than they should."

It sounded great to Max, but Lucy was biting her lip. "Um, I'm not sure I can really do that," she said hesitantly. "And I don't know how to get to anyone's house on my own. I can go back for Valentine, but I should probably let her rest up before school. . . ."

"No problem," Cami said quickly. "I was already thinking that you and I could go together. I'll look for visual clues and you can listen for clues. Or see if you can sniff any out." Cami smiled at her joke but Lucy's brow was tightly knit and the corners of her mouth turned down.

"I don't know, maybe I should just sit this part out," she said, so quietly Max could barely hear her over the sound of cars driving on the streets around the square.

"No, don't be silly," Cami said, sounding distressed. "We need you."

"Changes in voice pattern can indicate a lie," Max added. "You can be listening for that."

"And two people are more likely to pick up on subtle clues," Cami said, tossing Max a grateful look. "Like one person does the talking and the other keeps an ear out for anything unusual."

"Okay," Lucy said, but her shoulders were sagging.

Joe cleared his throat. "I'm not sure how much I can help," he said. Max turned just enough to see Joe scraping a line in the snow with the toe of his boot. "I don't know anyone on the list and I don't know what I'd say to them."

"You could try punching them," Max muttered. Joe lifted his head and gave Max a murderous look. Max glared back.

"That's why you'll go with Max," Cami said sweetly.

Max whipped his head around. Was she out of her mind? "What? No way."

"No," Joe echoed firmly.

Cami put a hand on her hip. "It makes the most sense," she said. "Like he said, Joe doesn't know anyone and Max, you know everyone. You can introduce Joe and then he can be on the lookout for clues while you get the conversation going."

"Not going to happen," Max said, and he meant it. But as he folded his arms over his chest, he could see that Cami was going to be just as stubborn.

She lifted her chin. "It makes the most sense," she repeated slowly, like she was talking to a baby.

Max glared at Cami. Clearly this had been her plan all along. Well, too bad. No way were Max and Joe going to spend the day together.

"If you really think it's the best way to get the job done, I'll do it," Joe said.

Max whipped around, his eyes blazing. What was wrong with Joe? Max knew Joe hated the idea as much as he did.

But Joe didn't even bother looking at Max. His shoulders slumped and he looked resigned, like the total and complete wimp he was.

Cami gave Max a smug smile.

Max threw up his arms, knowing defeat when it came his way. "Fine, whatever," he said.

"Great," Cami said in her regular voice, the sugar gone now that she'd gotten her way. She whipped out her phone. "I made a list of possible GBs."

Of course she had. Max leaned in so he could see the screen.

Mr. Pink

The VonWolfs

Alma Sanchez

The Barristers

"I was thinking that Lucy and I could go see Ms. Sanchez and you guys can visit the Barristers," Cami continued.

Max knew she was trying to make up for pairing him with Joe by suggesting they follow up on Max's favorite theory, but it was going to take a lot more than that for Max to forgive Cami.

"Remember to see if the Barristers have a lot of books to go with the bookmark." There was no guilt in Cami's voice and she had the gall to smile at them before she and Lucy headed off.

There was a long moment of silence after the girls left.

"So where are we going?" Joe asked lifelessly. Clearly he hated the thought of spending time with Max.

Max decided that just because they had to spend time together didn't mean they actually had to speak. So instead of answering, he headed off, leaving the square and heading down Church Street. Joe followed.

They walked four blocks, then turned on Market Street. Max glanced back, half hoping Joe had decided to go home, but he was still there, visibly shivering. Max realized that Joe's coat was way too thin for the bitter winters of Pine River. Joe's family probably didn't have much money for a new coat and Max was almost considering mentioning the church thrift shop, where his family got winter coats for him and Fiona every year. This year Max had gotten a nearly new Patagonia down jacket that was probably warm enough for camping out in the Himalayas. But before he could say anything, Joe caught his gaze and frowned.

"Problem?" he asked in his obnoxious way.

Max rolled his eyes and said nothing, just picked up his pace so they'd get this over with faster.

"What will we do when we get there?" Joe asked a few minutes later.

Max was tempted to keep on ignoring him but realized he needed to take charge of things or Joe would probably do something to mess the whole thing up.

"If they're home, we try to get them to talk," he said. "And if not, we'll take a quick look around, do some searching in their yard and peek in the windows."

"That sounds illegal," Joe said, sounding hesitant.

"You scared?" Max taunted.

Joe glared but he rose to the bait like Max knew he would. "Fine," he muttered.

The Barristers' house was on the corner of Market and Montgomery Streets, the only house on the block with a fence protecting the property. Their house was large, and kind of spooky, Max thought. It was painted a somber gray with black trim and the path hadn't been shoveled. The boys walked up the icy front steps and knocked. After a minute passed, Max knocked again.

"No one's here," Max announced when no one answered. He had to admit he was hoping for this. Getting either of the quiet Barristers to talk would be hard, so spying was really their best bet.

He peered into the window next to the door. He could see an entryway with a set of shelves for shoes and a closed door, probably a closet.

Joe hesitated, then glanced in. "Nothing here," he said. "Maybe we should leave."

"Let's go around back," Max said, ignoring Joe's annoying remark. They were going undercover, and Max was pumped up.

"What about our footprints?" Joe asked. "They'll know someone was here."

"But they won't know who," Max said cheerfully.

He pulled his hat down low over his eyes and wrapped his scarf around his face so that no one passing by would recognize him. Then he led the way around the house. The first window they peeked through showed a kitchen, full of the usual kitchen things. The dining room next door held a big wooden table but had only two chairs.

"I guess they don't have much company," Max said.

Joe shrugged and Max vowed not to talk to him again.

The next room was the living room, with a sagging sofa and chair set arranged around the fireplace. There was something slightly off about it but it took Max a minute to realize what it was.

"You know what's weird?" he asked, breaking his vow after only two minutes. He couldn't help it, though, not when he was in spy mode and uncovering so much. "They don't have any pictures up."

Joe's eyebrows scrunched. "I guess that's weird," he said. "They don't have any books either."

Max was irritated Joe had remembered to look out for that. "Maybe they have books in another room," he said, stepping away from the window and creeping around the corner of the house.

There was only one more set of windows. The little room at the end of the house was darker than the others, and it took Max's eyes a moment to adjust before he could make anything out. And when he did, none of it made sense. There was a framed photo of a young soldier posed in a fancy army uniform. Next to the picture was a set of dog tags, a stack of letters, and a velvet box. The rest of the room was empty.

Max started to say something about how strange it was when Joe, who had come up a moment later, gasped and stepped back from the window like something had bitten him.

"What's wrong?" Max asked.

Joe shook his head. He headed for the street, his jaw hard and his shoulders set.

Max followed, confused but also annoyed. "Do you know what that creepy room is?" he asked as he caught up to Joe.

"It's not creepy," Joe snapped in the snotty way that drove Max crazy.

"Yeah, it is," Max said defiantly. "Who has a room for one picture?"

Joe turned to him, eyes blazing. "You're an idiot," he said.

"At least I have friends and people actually like me," Max said, clenching his teeth and getting ready for a fight.

Joe glared a moment longer, then turned and started walking. "I'm going home," he said.

Max knew he should just let Joe go. His gut was boiling in a way that was dangerous, that let him know if he kept going he was going to get in trouble. But he couldn't just turn away, not this time.

"That's right," Max jeered. "Run home to your mama."

Joe stopped in his tracks and turned. "You don't talk about my mom," he said, his voice hard and low. "Not ever."

"Why, is she —" Max began, but then Joe moved toward him, a fist cocking back.

It wasn't the threat of being punched that shut Max up. It was the fact that Joe's eyes were full of tears.

"That room was a shrine for a fallen soldier," Joe said in a shaky voice. "A hero who died for his country. A hero like my mom."

"Wait, your mom's a soldier?" Max asked, shocked.

Joe nodded. "She's a marine," he said. "She's in the Middle East helping out with the peace initiative."

Max remembered what he had said way back in September that had made Joe haul off and punch him. It was about Joe's mom, a "your mama" joke, the kind the guys on the flag football team told all the time. And now, finally, Max got it: Joe's sullen silence, the way he kept to himself — he was worrying about his mom, who was far away and in constant danger. And that was the reason he had punched Max: He was defending his mom who was out defending their country. Max had just assumed Joe was a jerk when in fact Cami was right, Joe did have a story. And the only jerk in that story, the real story, was Max. Guilt began to seep into Max, a thick fog that made him feel about three inches tall.

"I'm sorry," he said.

"That my mom is in the armed forces?" Joe asked defensively. "Because —"

"No, for what I said just now," Max interrupted. "And for the joke I made in September." He scuffed his toe through the snow. "You're right. Your mom is a hero, and if she was here I'd want to thank her for what she's doing."

Joe shrugged, and for a second Max felt that rush of irritation, that Joe was just ignoring him again, but then he realized that Joe was swallowing hard.

A cold wind swirled around them and Max saw that Joe was shivering. "Let's go," he said, turning back toward town.

"Where?" Joe asked, his eyes narrowing.

"Do you have ten bucks on you?" Max asked, ignoring Joe's question.

"Um, yeah," Joe said. "Are you planning to blackmail me?"

Max laughed and shook his head. "We're going to the church thrift shop to get you a decent coat."

"My coat is fine," Joe said.

Max gave him a sharp look. "Do I really look like an idiot to you?" he asked. "You're miserable because that coat is useless in a real winter. And I know you don't think you're too good to get a coat where I get mine every year."

There was a long silence. Joe looked at Max, then off into the distance, then back at Max. "Okay," he said finally. "We can do that."

Max gave a firm nod and started back toward town.

"And, Max?"

He turned.

"Thanks," Joe said.

Chapter 16

Twelve Days until Christmas

T his place is huge," Cami said to Lucy as they walked up the icy path to Alma Sanchez's house. "I think she must have twenty-five rooms just for her and her cat."

"I bet the cat likes having the room to run around," Lucy said, trying to keep her voice light to hide how tired she was feeling. The walk to Ms. Sanchez's house wasn't more than a mile from Lucy's house but tromping through the fresh snow was taxing, especially since sometimes there were ice patches or uneven sections of the sidewalk that were easy to trip on. Plus there was the stress of knowing she was slowing Cami down. Right about now Lucy was really missing Valentine.

Cami laughed as she led them up the steps. Lucy snagged the toe of her boot on the first one — it was always hard to gauge how high steps were — but Cami had her arm and she steadied herself. Cami shifted slightly to ring the bell, which Lucy heard chime inside the home. A minute later the door flew open.

"Cami, Lucy, come in," Ms. Sanchez said.

Cami guided Lucy into a warm room that smelled of butter cookies and pine needles. If the house was as big as Cami claimed, Lucy imagined that the Christmas tree must be spectacular.

"Perfect timing!" Ms. Sanchez said. "I'm testing a Christmas cookie recipe. You'll have to try some and tell me what you think."

"If you insist," Cami said in her usual friendly way.

"Thanks," Lucy added.

"You girls make yourselves at home and I'll be right back with the cookies," Ms. Sanchez said.

"Here's the sofa," Cami said, carefully backing Lucy up so that her calves rested against the seat. "And just so you know, this whole room is lined with bookcases. She's definitely a big reader."

"So the bookmark could belong to her," Lucy said, sinking down on the soft cushions.

"Yeah, she fits a lot of the profile. She's a reader, she has money and time . . ." Cami said in a low voice.

"Plus she's generous, inviting us in without even asking why we're here," Lucy added.

"I know," Cami agreed. "She reminds me of my grandma, always welcoming."

Lucy noticed a note of sadness in Cami's voice and wondered if she should ask about it, but then she heard footsteps coming down the hall toward them and a moment later Ms. Sanchez was back, the smell of cookies even more powerful.

"Lucy, here's your plate," Ms. Sanchez said, handing it to Lucy and making sure she had it securely before letting go. "How's that dog of yours?"

At this Lucy smiled, remembering how kind Ms. Sanchez had been on the street that day. "She's great, thanks," Lucy said. Lucy waited until she heard Cami crunching into her cookie, then she felt for hers. It was in the shape of a candy cane and studded with rough sugar sprinkles. Lucy took a bite, the luscious buttery cookie just the right amount of sweet. "Delicious," she said when she had swallowed.

"Mm-hm," Cami agreed. "These are fantastic."

"Thank you," Ms. Sanchez said, sounding pleased. "Oh, are either of you allergic to cats? I think Naomi is coming in to pay a visit."

Lucy shook her head, and a moment later she heard a soft thump as the cat jumped up on the sofa and came over to sniff Lucy's hand, her whiskers soft against Lucy's skin. Lucy let Naomi sniff her for a moment, then began to pet her. Naomi kneaded her paws into the sofa and started to purr.

"She likes you," Ms. Sanchez said.

Lucy smiled. "I like her too," she said.

"She's beautiful," Cami said, reaching over to pet Naomi as well.

Then Lucy felt Cami shift slightly on the sofa and knew she was about to bring up the excuse they'd planned for knocking on Ms. Sanchez's door in the first place. "So we came by because we know you lead the town choir Christmas caroling on December twenty-first and I had kind of a special request for when you come by our place. My grandmother's favorite carol is

'Go Tell It on the Mountain' and I was wondering if you guys could sing it for her."

"I'd be happy to," Ms. Sanchez said. "And how thoughtful of you to think of it." Lucy heard her pick up another cookie.

"Well, she does a lot for me," Cami said. "And she just loves everything about Christmas in Pine River."

"Don't we all," Ms. Sanchez said.

Now it was Lucy's turn and she sat up a little straighter, accidentally startling the cat. "I love the Christmas Gala." She tried to make her rehearsed line sound natural, but she felt like her voice was coming out stiff. "Every year the concert is just amazing." Lucy tried again. "Totally amazing." She was glad Max was not here to see her total spy fail.

"We'll all be looking forward to your part in that," Ms. Sanchez said to Cami.

Lucy was surprised when Cami said nothing, but she pressed on with the script. "And of course there's the Angel Tree," she said, like it had just in that moment occurred to her.

"Yeah, it's already granted some pretty incredible wishes," Cami added.

"Like the new house for the Callahans," Ms. Sanchez said. "Ed Pink was telling me about it. Wow, imagine all the work it would take to set up such a thing."

Of course whoever was behind the tree would pretend to be impressed by it, to hide his or her tracks. Lucy listened intently for any inflections that might indicate Ms. Sanchez was hiding something. But either Ms. Sanchez wasn't GB, or she was a much better actor than Lucy.

"The person behind the tree is truly an angel," Ms. Sanchez went on passionately. "A maker of miracles."

Lucy heard Cami slump slightly next to her and had to admit that this wasn't sounding good. Yes, GB would cover the truth but he or she probably wouldn't go around boasting about the work the tree did.

"We're lucky to live in a town with a person who would create such a special and unique tradition," Ms. Sanchez said. "It's a blessing."

Lucy sank back deeper into the sofa cushions. They could probably cross Ms. Sanchez off the list of possible GBs.

"Girls, is everything okay?" Ms. Sanchez asked.

Lucy realized she had let her face fall into a frown. She was definitely not good at hiding her true feelings.

"No, it's just, we're kind of on a mission to find out who's behind the Angel Tree," Cami said.

"Isn't the whole point of the Angel Tree that the identity of the organizer is a secret?" Ms. Sanchez asked.

"Yes," Cami said. "But whoever is behind the tree has been doing it for so many years and has never been thanked. We wanted to change that."

There was a tiny rustle that was either Ms. Sanchez shaking her head or nodding. Sometimes not being able to see was frustrating.

"You know, I like that idea," Ms. Sanchez said. "The person bringing so much joy to our town should get some joy coming back her way."

So she had been nodding.

"Her?" Cami asked, her voice suddenly alert. "You think it's a woman?"

Ms. Sanchez laughed. "You're quite the detective. Well, I'm not sure. But every so often when I help out with a bigger wish I get a handwritten note and the writing looks like a woman's writing."

"Do you have a note?" Cami asked eagerly.

"I do," Ms. Sanchez said. Lucy could hear the smile in her voice as she stood up and opened a drawer in a desk or table at the far side of the room. "Here you go," she said, walking back and handing it to Cami.

Cami cleared her throat. "Okay, this is what it says: 'Please give your donated ornaments to Ed Pink on Saturday afternoon.'"

"Not a lot to get from that, I don't think," Ms. Sanchez said.

"No, but the writing is very, um, curly," Cami said, clearly trying to stay positive. "It kind of looks like my grandma's."

Ms. Sanchez laughed. "That would be quite the mystery to uncover — your own grandmother being the one behind the Angel Tree."

Cami laughed. "She would totally do something like that, but there's no way she could keep it a secret from me." Her voice had a little of its bounce back, but Lucy could tell she was still discouraged that Ms. Sanchez was not GB. And Lucy had to admit she felt the same. She rubbed Naomi's head, feeling slightly comforted by the cat's steady purr.

"We should probably get going," Cami said, her coat brushing against the sofa as she stood.

They thanked Ms. Sanchez for the cookies, gave Naomi one last pat, and began the trip back to town.

"Ruling people out is an important part of the process," Cami said as they walked. Lucy was starting to know Cami well enough that she could tell that the upbeat, adult tone covered her disappointment.

"It is," Lucy agreed staunchly. "And what's good is that we found out so fast that it's not Ms. Sanchez. That way we're not wasting time on a false lead. Plus the note is a great clue."

"Good point," Cami said a bit more cheerfully. "It really did look like a woman's writing, so we can include that on our list of traits."

A car drove past slowly and the driver honked. "It's Ms. Clayton," Cami said, waving at one of the owners of Hobby Horse, a craft shop in town. Lucy waved too. "That reminds me, actually," Cami went on. "I wanted to get some yarn for my grandmother. She's crocheting a scarf for my cousin Willa." Lucy heard a note of tension when Cami said her cousin's name. "And she needs more gold. Would you mind if we stopped off at the Hobby Horse before I take you home?"

"No, that's fine," Lucy said. She would have preferred to go straight home and rest but of course she was happy to make the stop for Cami. If she had more energy, she'd get some yarn for the sweater she was knitting her mom for Christmas but right now the thought of a long conversation about getting just the right shade of green made her want to take a nap.

A few minutes later they were back on Main Street and Cami was opening the door to the Hobby Horse, which smelled of lavender and wool. "Do you mind if I run in and get the yarn?" Cami asked.

"Sure, I'll just wait here," Lucy said. The store was crowded with voices and smells, and Lucy felt a headache tapping at her temples. She stepped backward and felt her hip brush against something that fell to the floor with a series of loud crashes. Someone gave out a small cry and a number of people gasped. Lucy's whole body clenched up as she waited to hear what had happened, what she had done.

"Don't worry, it's fine." It was Ms. Clayton, still smelling like the crisp outside air. "Just be careful you don't hurt yourself, Lucy."

Lucy didn't know what she meant or how exactly she was supposed to protect herself. She felt naked and helpless, like a baby unable to do the simplest thing. It did not help when Cami came up sounding panicked.

"Lucy, I'm so sorry I left you so close to that display," Cami said, grabbing onto Lucy's arm and walking her away from whatever mess she had created. "I wasn't even thinking about how delicate it was and how easy it would be to knock into it."

"What was it?" Lucy asked, feeling close to tears.

"Um, some crystal figurines and a couple of glass vases," Cami said.

"And they're all broken?" Lucy asked, shame flooding her.

"I'm not sure," Cami said distractedly. Of course she didn't want to be explaining every little detail to Lucy when she was probably angry at her for being so careless.

"I'm so sorry," Lucy said, but her words were lost in the sounds of a vacuum turning on and the clinky whoosh of the shards of glass and crystal being sucked up.

Cami apologized to Ms. Clayton about a thousand times, which only made Lucy feel worse. After all, it wasn't Cami's fault that Lucy was a klutz. Finally Cami took Lucy's arm and walked them out into the icy air that cooled Lucy's hot face.

"I'm really sorry," Lucy said as Cami led her home.

"Don't worry, it wasn't your fault," Cami said, but she sounded distant.

"It was, actually," Lucy said, her voice brittle. "And I'm sorry you didn't get the yarn either."

"Really, Lucy it's all fine," Cami said. Lucy thought she detected a note of impatience in Cami's voice and decided to let it drop, even though the whole thing felt like a lump of coal in her belly.

They walked the rest of the way to Lucy's in silence.

Once she was up in her room, Lucy lay down on her bed. She had a message from Anya but she didn't feel like calling her friend back now. She wasn't in the mood to talk to anyone. At least not any person.

Instead she rested her cheek against Valentine's soft fur. "It was a mistake for me to go," she told the dog, whose tail thumped on the floor when she heard Lucy's voice. "I made everything harder, just like I knew I would." She rubbed Valentine's ears and was rewarded with a lick on her hand.

Lucy was thankful that Valentine would be back at school with her on Monday, and still endlessly grateful to the person behind the Angel Tree, who had saved her dog's life. Which was the only reason she was going to go to the meetings after school. But from here on out, no matter how bad it made her feel, she was going to be firm: no more outings where she would make a mess of things.

Chapter 17

Eleven Days until Christmas

Cami picked at the grilled cheese on the plate in front of her, if you could call it that. She'd tried to make lunch, but ended up with a charred crisp of a sandwich. She could hear her grandmother in the other room, chatting on the phone with her aunt about Willa's latest accomplishment. Worst of all, Cami couldn't stop thinking about what had happened with Lucy. And she had no idea how to apologize without making Lucy feel even worse.

A moment later her grandmother popped her head in. "I need to pick up a few things at the grocery," her grandmother said. "Come along and keep me company."

The last thing Cami felt like doing was heading out to the crowded market, but she knew her grandmother needed help with the heavy bags of food. Maybe she could finally get *something* right this weekend. So she headed downstairs, put on her boots, and got into her grandmother's ancient Honda.

"You're awfully quiet," her grandmother said as she backed the car down their driveway. "Everything okay?"

"Yeah," Cami said. "I just have a lot of homework."

"Still taking that break from the violin?" her grandmother asked.

Cami's chest tightened. "Um, yeah," she said. She never lied to her grandmother and you could maybe argue that this wasn't a complete lie. Still, it was stretching the truth till it felt like something else entirely. But Cami wanted to tell her grandmother the big change she had made when it was actually worth talking about — when she had used her new free time to do something truly Willa-worthy. And so far that had not happened.

Her grandmother glanced at her for a moment and Cami steeled herself for more questions. But her grandmother stayed quiet.

She wouldn't have believed it was possible, but now Cami felt even worse. Her grandmother had said nothing about missing hearing her play or how Cami needed to prepare for the Christmas Gala. It was almost as though she were glad Cami wasn't playing. Which shouldn't have been a surprise considering the conversation she had had with Willa's mom, but still hit Cami like a sharp jab at the soft part of her belly.

The grocery store was crowded and the lights felt harsh. Cami steered the cart as her grandmother filled it up with pasta, juice, and bread. There was a long line at the meat counter and Cami leaned on the cart as her grandmother chatted with a church friend waiting in front of them. But then she saw something that made her stand up straight: Mrs. VonWolf, the tiny old lady huffing as she pushed a cart filled to the brim with food. Behind her came her husband, barely an inch taller and pushing a cart piled even higher, if that was possible.

There was no way they were going to eat all that food. They had to be buying it for someone else. Possibly someone who had made a wish on the Angel Tree.

Cami crept up behind them to see what was in their carts. Both were piled high with Fruity Frosted Crunch cereal, chocolate granola bars, boxes of macaroni and cheese, and several big bottles of fruit punch. All food a ten-year-old would like, not an elderly couple.

"So we'll just box this up and get it to the Naylors' house when Ed Pink delivers their tree at seven," Mr. VonWolf was saying, running a hand through his sparse white hair.

The Naylors lived on the edge of town and Mr. Naylor had been out of work for almost a year. Cami knew the only way they could afford Christmas for their three young kids was with a little help from the Angel Tree.

"Perfect," his wife said. "We just need to grab some staples for the parents and I think we're set."

"And you said Alma Sanchez is taking care of the gifts?" Mr. VonWolf asked as they headed down the aisle.

Cami wasn't tired or low anymore. This was a clue, and a fantastic one at that! The VonWolfs were helping out with an important wish and they were also obviously the ones organizing it. After all, how else could they know that Mr. Pink was delivering the tree and Alma Sanchez was taking care of the gifts?

Cami couldn't wait to call Joe, Lucy, and Max the second she got home and tell them they had new prime candidates for GB!

✴

Chapter 18

Eleven Days
until Christmas

Max was walking home from a hockey game when Cami called, giving him the low-down on her trip to Ms. Sanchez's and her intel on the VonWolfs.

"The note is a great clue," Max said, feeling pumped up by the game and now the new lead on GB. "And that was some good spying on the VonWolfs."

"The VonWolfs are definitely on the top of the list," Cami said, ignoring his spy comment. "Mrs. VonWolf could easily be the person who writes out all the notes. I was thinking we should go talk to them tomorrow after school."

"Sounds good," Max said. "I'll be there." His skate bag was starting to slide off his shoulder, so he hitched it up.

"Great," Cami said. "Now I just have to figure out how to tell Joe. I don't have his phone number."

Max sighed. It was time to hear Cami say, *I told you so.*

"I'll tell Joe," Max said.

"Wait, what?" Cami asked, her shock like an electric current through the phone.

"I wouldn't go so far as to say you were *right*, but he's not a bad guy," Max said. He held the phone away from his ear so that he wouldn't have to hear Cami shout, *I told you so.* When he brought it back a moment later, she was still talking.

". . . So I *was* right, wasn't I? And it turns out my idea for you guys to go to the Barristers' was a good one, wasn't it? I knew it!" She paused. "What happened there, anyway? Did you find anything?"

Max sobered as he told Cami about the shrine. He had just come into the main square and seeing the Angel Tree, so filled with hope, somehow made the sad Barrister house feel even more awful.

"Maybe we can do something for them," Cami said.

Max could practically hear the wheels in her head spinning away on a new project. "Yeah, we could . . ." he said. "But I still wonder if they're GB. Maybe after they lost their son they decided to do something good like he did, and they started the Angel Tree. I know the VonWolfs look like they're the prime suspects but I don't think we can eliminate the Barristers."

"They're not suspects," Cami said with an eye roll Max could hear in her voice. "But you're right that we should still consider them. Go tell your new best friend, Joe, that we're meeting up to check on the VonWolfs tomorrow."

After signing off, Max shoved his phone in his pocket. He realized he didn't actually have Joe's number but he remembered that Joe had mentioned living over the Lost Sock Laundromat, and that was only a few blocks away so Max figured he'd just drop by. He stopped on the corner of Montgomery and Main while Mr. Pink drove by, honking and waving as he went. As Max waved back, he noticed a bunch of new basketball supplies piled in the back of Mr. Pink's pickup truck. It was probably another Angel Tree wish. The VonWolfs and the Barristers were definitely top suspects but Mr. Pink was still in the race.

The Lost Sock Laundromat had a lone dryer spinning on the back wall when Max walked in and began searching for a way to get to the second floor. He finally found it outside, a small door on the side of the building, and headed up the narrow staircase, noticing that the steps were coated with dust and the paint on the walls was chipped. The excitement he felt at Cami's news began to curdle into something that felt more like worry as he knocked on the door. A few moments later, he heard footsteps and then Joe opened the door.

"Hey," Joe said, smiling when he realized it was Max. "I think this is the first time anyone's knocked on the door since I moved in here. Come on in."

Max walked into the apartment. "We're going to investigate the VonWolfs tomorrow," he said. His voice trailed off as he looked around at the place where his friend lived. There was a sagging leather sofa, an ancient Barcalounger, and a rickety table off to one side. The carpet was stained, the walls were bare, and the only thing that looked truly clean was the large television standing on a flimsy black plastic stand. As he took it all in, Max noticed a mass under the table and for a moment thought it was some kind of body bag. But then reality checked in and he realized it was a sleeping bag. "You camp out?" he asked.

Joe cleared his throat. "My uncle doesn't have another bedroom, so I sleep in here."

"But why can't you sleep on the sofa?" Max asked. He had a vague sense that he was being rude, but his shock at seeing how Joe lived had robbed him of his manners.

"My uncle watches TV pretty late sometimes," Joe said quietly. "It's easier to block it out and get to sleep if I'm over here."

"That's just wrong," Max blurted out.

"It's fine," Joe said in the same quiet voice. "Can I get you anything to drink? I was going to make some cocoa."

"Sure," Max said, still not able to understand why Joe had to sleep under a table.

He followed his friend into the kitchen, where there was a half-size fridge and some shelves that were empty save for a few packs of ramen, some cans of soup, and a big box of saltines. A microwave took up most of the scratched counter and when he looked around, Max noticed a big patch of mold on one wall. He wouldn't have believed it possible but he had actually stumbled into a place that made his family's current apartment seem like a palace.

Max looked at his friend, who was carefully scrubbing out two mugs, and something twisted in his chest. "I can't believe this is where you live," he said.

Joe's shoulders stiffened but when he turned to face Max he didn't look angry or sad or anything that Max knew he would be feeling if he stood in Joe's shoes. "Leon was the only one who could take me in while my mom served," he said simply. "And dealing with this is nothing compared to what she's dealing with over there."

Max had always thought of himself as tough, able to laugh off accidental hits in football or fight hard for the puck in hockey. He'd broken his leg, gotten stitches twice, and hadn't cried when the neighbor's dog bit him so deep he had to go to the hospital. But standing next to Joe and his quiet pride, Max felt like a complete cream puff, a pampered, spoiled kid who had always been taken care of, no matter what.

He wanted to tell Joe that what he was doing was pretty incredible, that if he were in Joe's shoes he'd never handle it this well. But words like that didn't come easily to Max. Instead he slapped Joe on the back and said, "So where's that cocoa?"

And Joe smiled as he dried off the mugs and began to prepare their drinks.

Chapter 19

***

Ten Days
until Christmas

When the final bell rang, Cami headed to her locker, taking the long way down the back hall so she wouldn't pass the music room. She quickly dialed her locker combination. The four of them had plans to meet at the front door and head over to the VonWolfs and she was eager to get going.

As she piled books into her backpack, Cami thought about how much Joe had changed. After she'd spoken to Max on Sunday, Cami had realized that her plan to help Joe make friends and find his place in Pine River was a success. But somehow when she went downstairs to tell her grandmother about it, the words wouldn't come. Somewhere along the line, Joe had become a friend instead of a project. To boast about helping him felt wrong. Though of course that put the pressure on for finding GB, so Cami had fingers and toes crossed that they were going to uncover the truth today.

She pulled on her coat and swung her heavy backpack over her shoulders.

Max, Joe, Lucy, and Valentine were already waiting at the exit.

"Ready?" Max asked, bouncing a little as he spoke. Clearly he was itching to get on with the investigation.

Joe and Cami started toward the door but then Lucy cleared her throat.

"You guys, I'm going to sit this one out," she said quietly.

"Why?" Cami demanded, her eyes narrowing.

Lucy let out a long breath and bent down to rub Valentine's head, as though that would help her answer. "You know why," she said quietly. "I slow you guys down and make everything harder."

Cami's eyes were blazing. "Not true," she said, almost angrily.

"It is," Lucy said. "I take twice as long to walk anywhere we go and —"

"But you have Valentine back," Cami interrupted. "And even if you didn't, no one cares if it takes us five extra minutes to get somewhere."

"And you have to take care of me," Lucy said. Her lips trembled the tiniest bit after she spoke.

"What happened at Hobby Horse was my fault," Cami said, guilt from that day pricking at the back of her neck.

"How could it have been your fault?" Lucy asked. "You were halfway across the store." Her voice was sharp.

"Because I left you somewhere that wasn't safe," Cami said, frustrated. "And I didn't let you know what was around you."

"That's the whole point!" Lucy exploded. "You have to take care of me."

"Whoa," Max said, waving his arms. "Time-out. What is going on?"

Both Cami and Lucy began to speak at once.

"It doesn't matter," Joe said quickly. "What matters is that we want your help, Lucy."

"Joe's right," Max said. "Accidents happen. Believe me, I know. But you think of stuff the rest of us could never come up with. We need you."

Cami beamed at the boys, beyond grateful for their words. Then she turned to Lucy. "So please say you'll come," she said softly.

Lucy sighed and Cami could see that she was torn. But finally she nodded. "Okay, I'll come."

Cami sighed in relief as they finally headed out, all four of them, just like it should be.

It was a gray afternoon with dusty clouds hanging low and thick; it was going to snow soon for sure.

"So what are we telling the VonWolfs?" Max asked, pulling his blue wool hat down over his ears. "We need a reason for showing up at their door."

"Right," Cami said, fishing around in her pockets for her gloves. She was worried she had left them back at school. "We thought we'd just say that our homework for the week is helping out neighbors, kind of a good Samaritan thing for the holidays. And we wanted to know if they need any help."

"Like with shoveling snow," Joe said as the first flakes began to fall.

"Exactly," Cami said. Her gloves weren't there and her hands were already starting to feel icy. She stuffed them deep in her pockets.

"I wonder if there's a way we can get a look at Mrs. VonWolf's handwriting," Joe said thoughtfully. "Then we could see if it matched the note you saw."

"Good idea," Cami exclaimed. "Is there a way we could ask her to sign something?"

"Or maybe we could do a little spying," Max said eagerly. "Like make an excuse to go to the kitchen to see a grocery list on the fridge or something."

"Or Christmas cards on a desk . . ." Joe added, clearly as into the spying as Max, which made Cami roll her eyes. Still, unless she could think of something to ask Mrs. VonWolf to sign, it was probably their best bet.

The VonWolfs lived in a big Victorian house on Fisher Lane. They had a large yard with flower beds, bushes, and a small fish pond that was frozen over. Most of the yard was piled high with snowdrifts, but the stone path leading up to the front porch was fully cleared. Cami headed up the stairs first, followed by Lucy with Valentine and then the boys.

Cami was about to ring the bell when the door flew open.

"Oh," cried Mrs. VonWolf, putting a hand to her heart. "You scared me. I had no idea anyone was out here."

"I'm so sorry," Cami said. This was off to a terrible start.

But then Mrs. VonWolf began to laugh. "I fear I'm getting hard of hearing in my old age," she said. "We were just going to run a few errands but it's delightful to see all of you." She smoothed a lock of silver hair that had fallen free of her bun.

"Can we help with the errands at all?" Cami asked. "That's actually why we're here. This week the kids in our class are going around town seeing if there are ways we can help people."

"Well, isn't that a lovely holiday activity," Mrs. VonWolf said. "And as a matter of fact, you *could* help us load a few of these boxes if it isn't too much trouble." She stood back and gestured to a stack of cardboard boxes, each one carefully labeled.

Cami immediately scanned the writing, to see if it looked like the writing on the note Alma Sanchez had shown her. But each box was scrawled with big block let-ters. It was impossible to tell what the handwriting would be on a note.

But then Cami actually read what the labels said and her heart began to race. *Christmas stockings for the Washington family. Football equipment for the Martin brothers. Year supply of cat food for Helen Zinn.* These were Angel Tree wishes, she was sure of it!

"We'd be happy to help with those, Mrs. VonWolf," Max said, stepping forward. "And this is Joe. He's new to town."

"Hello, Joe," Mrs. VonWolf said as her husband came up behind her. He was completely bald but made up for it with a shaggy white beard. "Herman, these young people are going to help us load the boxes. And this fellow, Joe, is new to Pine River."

"Nice to meet you," Mr. VonWolf said, pumping Joe's hand.

"Nice to meet you too, sir," Joe said.

"We sure do appreciate your help," Mr. VonWolf said as Max grabbed the first box. "Let me just get the trunk of the car open." He grabbed his coat from the rack in the entryway and then headed carefully down the stairs, Max and Joe following with boxes.

"I'm sorry I can't help with the boxes," Lucy said in a small voice. Cami realized that Lucy still had no idea that the boxes were Angel Tree wishes but there was no way to tell her with Mrs. VonWolf standing right there. She hated seeing how left out her friend looked.

"Oh, sweetie, not to worry," Mrs. VonWolf said, putting an arm around Lucy. "Let the boys do the heavy lifting."

Lucy managed a small smile.

"Good idea," Cami said a little too forcefully. Being anxious always made her pushy and she took a breath before continuing. "I mean, I'm sure they can take care of it just fine."

"You girls come in and warm up for a moment," Mrs. VonWolf said. "It's really starting to come down out there."

Cami glanced back and saw that the snow was falling thick and fast now. "Thanks," she said.

They handed their coats to Mrs. VonWolf, who hung them up and then led the girls into a living room filled with velvet armchairs, several floral-printed love seats, and two plush sofas. There were several low side tables scattered around the large room and a thick carpet covered most of the floor. Best of all, there were two wide floor-to-ceiling bookcases crammed with books. Cami went through their checklist in her head. A reader, check. Someone with enough money, check. She could barely keep her excitement in — it was looking more and more like the VonWolfs were GB!

Just then Lucy, who was following Valentine, tripped over the edge of the carpet and hit her shin against one of the tables before catching her balance.

"Lucy, are you all right?" Mrs. VonWolf asked, rushing over to help.

"I'm fine, thank you," Lucy said. Cami heard the dismay in her voice and her chest squeezed. "I hope I didn't damage anything."

"Not at all," Mrs. VonWolf said.

Lucy sat down, but Cami saw that her hands were shaky. "I wanted to thank you for how you've been helping us get Valentine's medication."

"I'm glad we've been able to do it," Mrs. VonWolf said. "We opened a drugstore to help people and it brings us great pleasure to do so." She stood up. "Cami, if it isn't too much trouble, would you help me get the last few boxes out of the kitchen?"

This was her big chance to find a handwriting sample! Cami jumped to her feet. She felt bad leaving Lucy when she was clearly upset, but Cami knew it would be worth it if they could confirm that the VonWolfs were indeed GB.

The kitchen was painted a cheerful yellow and was perfumed by the smell of recently baked gingerbread that Mrs. VonWolf had been putting in big tins printed with colorful Christmas trees and candy canes.

"I'll just take these if you could get the other two," Mrs. Von Wolf said, picking up three of the tins.

"Sure," Cami said, her eyes darting around the kitchen for any signs of handwriting. There was nothing on the spotless countertops but the fridge had a number of papers stuck to it with magnets.

Cami thought fast. "Is it okay if I just get a quick glass of water?" she asked. "My throat is really dry from the cold." She gave a small fake cough, which turned quickly into a real coughing fit.

"Oh, let me get you something," Mrs. VonWolf said, turning.

"No!" Cami choked out a little too loudly. "I mean," she went on more quietly. "I can get it myself and then I'll bring out the tins."

"Okay, dear," Mrs. VonWolf said.

The second she was out the door, Cami raced over to the fridge. There were a few Christmas cards from friends and family. No good. Then Cami spotted a grocery list. She bent forward to look more closely. The writing was definitely curly, but was it the same kind of curly as the note Ms. Sanchez had showed her? Cami wasn't sure.

"Did you find the glasses?" Mrs. VonWolf called from the hall.

"Yes, thank you," Cami said. She froze. She knew she had to hurry, but she couldn't decide if the writing was the same. Finally, she grabbed the list off the fridge and stuffed it in her pocket. It was stuck to a Christmas card, so Cami ended up taking that too.

"Thanks for the help, kids," Mr. VonWolf said as Cami carried the tins of gingerbread into the hall. "We should get those boxes delivered now before the driving conditions get too bad."

Cami and Lucy put their coats back on and the four of them headed out into the snowy afternoon.

"So did you guys find anything out?" Max asked.

Lucy shook her head but Cami bit her lip. "Um, I stole a shopping list," she said.

Max hooted. "You need help deciding what to have for dinner?"

"Very funny. I took it for the writing sample."

"Cami, I didn't think you had it in you," Max said, slapping her on the back. "But it turns out you're real spy material. I'm so proud."

She rolled her eyes. "We'll see if it helps." They stopped at a bench and she pulled the list and the card out of her pocket.

"What's that?" Joe asked.

"I accidently grabbed one of their Christmas cards too." Cami hoped it wasn't from someone special. She handed it to Joe to free her hands, then held out the list.

"So is the writing the same?" Lucy asked.

Cami stared at it. "It's really hard to tell," she said. "I mean, it's curly but I can't tell if it's curly in the same way as the note."

Max immediately grinned. "Sounds like we need to get that note from Alma Sanchez and do a real comparison."

"Um, actually I'm not sure if we'll need to," Joe said in a low voice. He was staring at the card in his hand.

"What do you mean?" Lucy asked.

"I just read the Christmas card that you took. It's from the Pinks. And here it says, 'We've been proud to call you members of our community for the past twelve years,'" he read, then looked up at Cami. "Didn't you say that the Angel Tree has been a tradition for twenty-five years?"

Cami's hopeful feeling popped like a balloon. "Yeah," she said, sighing.

"So if the VonWolfs only moved here twelve years ago, they couldn't be GB," Joe finished gloomily.

"I guess we have to cross them off the list," Max said.

"Looks like it," Cami said reluctantly. She knew they still had two other possibilities on their list, Mr. Pink and the Barristers, but she'd really been convinced that the VonWolfs were GB.

Joe and Max walked ahead as they started back toward town.

"Are you okay?" Cami asked Lucy as they trudged through the snowdrifts that were beginning to pile up on the sidewalk.

Lucy nodded. "Yeah, just a little tired."

Cami knew it was more than that but she didn't push. Sometimes you just needed to feel bad for a bit, without someone trying to cheer you up.

Which was exactly how Cami herself was feeling.

That evening Cami was slumped on the floor in the middle of her room. Her homework was spread out in front of her, but she couldn't focus on it at all. Normally when she felt this down she would play her violin. Concentrating on the notes or on the complicated fingerings could clear her mind of anything else. But that wasn't an option now.

She sighed and started sorting through the pile of clothes on the floor of her messy closet. At least cleaning her room would please her grandmother. When she was done there, she started in on the top of her dresser. It was piled high with hair bands, jewelry, and tubes of lip gloss. Digging through, Cami found a chunk of rosin, the powder used to get the best sound out of a violin bow. She sadly tucked it away into a drawer. Then, underneath all the mess, she came across the bookmark they had found at Pine Forest.

She picked it up carefully. The leather had dried and it was stiff in her hands. The ivy carving was more pronounced and when she flipped it over Cami saw something that had been invisible when the bookmark was swollen with water: two letters. *RB*. Initials?

With growing excitement, she realized that one of the possible GB's on the list had a last name that started with B: the Barristers. What if Max was right and the whole time they had been hiding out in their home while secretly giving the town the greatest gift ever?

Cami dug around on her desk until she found her cell phone. News like this could not wait until the morning. And the first person she was calling was Lucy. This was the best possible way to move on from the bad afternoon: a new lead!

Chapter 20

Nine Days
until Christmas

"Hi, Lucy," Joe said as he walked into the library after the last bell of the day had rung. Lucy was standing at Ms. Marwich's desk. He smiled when he saw the librarian. He'd been meaning to tell her about how the Angel Tree had helped him. "Hi, Ms. Marwich."

"Good afternoon," Ms. Marwich said. "I was just telling Lucy how nice it is to see Valentine back and doing so well."

"I'm really happy she's okay," Lucy said with a smile. And then Joe saw her frown the tiniest bit. "What about Tango? Is he okay?"

Joe wondered if something had happened to Ms. Marwich's cat. He hoped not, knowing how much Ms. Marwich cared about him.

But Ms. Marwich just looked confused. "What do you mean?" she asked.

"Oh, I just thought — never mind," Lucy said.

Joe could see that Lucy was uncomfortable. "We should see if Max and Cami are here," he said to her, figuring he could thank Ms. Marwich for her advice later.

"I believe the rest of your outfit awaits in the back room," Ms. Marwich said. "Good luck with world domination."

"I thought Ms. Marwich smelled like the vet's office," Lucy said as they walked back, Valentine leading the way. "I guess I was wrong, but it's weird. That smell is pretty distinctive."

"Maybe it's a doctor's office or something," Joe said. He hoped nothing was wrong with Ms. Marwich.

Max and Cami were already at the table when they walked in. Cami was looking at the suspect list on her phone but by now Joe knew it by heart. Alma Sanchez and the VonWolfs were out and the two remaining possibilities were Mr. Pink and the Barristers. Joe didn't want to think about what might happen if neither turned out to be GB. But then again the Barristers looked nearly certain, so there was probably nothing to worry about.

"Should we go try to talk to the Barristers today?" Max asked. He was clearly ready to jump into spy mode and Joe felt the same. He was eager to solve this mystery once and for all.

Cami shook her head as she slipped her phone into her pocket. "I talked to my grandma about them last night and she said that Mrs. Barrister is always at her Friday-afternoon bingo game at church. I think we have a way better chance of getting her to talk there, when she's out already, then just showing up on her doorstep. So that means today we get to check out the Pinks."

"Let's do it," Max said, pushing back his chair and gathering his stuff.

The day was bright and sunny but fiercely cold as they headed out of school and into town, and Joe felt grateful for his warm new coat. Main Street, with its glittering Christmas lights and festive decorations, felt familiar to Joe now, and he paused to look in the window of Bits of the Past, an antique store where there was an old-fashioned chess set with pieces that were clearly hand carved. Seeing it made him think of Ariana and the chess club and he realized it had been a while since he'd thought about his old school.

"That jacket would look awesome on you," Max said from behind him, pointing at the bright red velvet jacket on display.

Joe gave him a withering look as the girls giggled. "I was looking at the chess set," he said.

Cami's eyes widened. "You play chess?" she asked.

"Yeah," he said as they began walking again. "Do you?" It would be fun to have someone to play with in Pine River, even if Joe's chess set just had plastic pieces, nothing like the ones in the store.

Cami shook her head vigorously. "Um, not really my thing," she said, looking like she was going to start laughing again.

Joe looked at Max, who just raised his eyebrows and shook his head, clearly thinking the same thing Joe was: Sometimes girls were really weird.

Outside Handyman Hardware, Cami turned to the others and opened her mouth.

"We know, we know," Max said before she could speak. "Try to steer the conversation toward the Angel Tree or books."

Joe couldn't help adding, "And see if we can get them to admit their last name is really Bink instead of Pink."

For a moment he worried Cami might be offended but instead she burst out laughing and Joe's cheeks warmed with pleasure. He'd forgotten how fun it was to joke around like this.

Max gave Joe a high five, then opened the door to Handyman Hardware and led the way inside.

It was crowded. Joe saw Mr. Pink up on a ladder pulling out a box of nails. They edged their way to the counter, where two salespeople were ringing up customers. Mrs. Pink stood behind them, talking on the phone.

"Yes," she was saying. "We'll be getting those in on the twentieth. How's that?"

Valentine yelped as someone stepped on her tail and Lucy knelt to comfort her. Cami shot Max and Joe a look. This was not a good time to investigate — the store was way too busy.

But then Mr. Pink caught sight of them. "Hey, kids," he said as he stepped off the ladder and tucked the nails into a box on the counter. "I'm heading out on an errand for the Angel Tree but let me get someone to help you."

Joe tried to think of something he might need to buy but Cami was two steps ahead.

"My grandmother needs a new hammer," she said. "And I think it's great you're doing something for the Angel Tree."

Mr. Pink nodded absently as he looked around for a free salesperson to help with the hammer. "Yep, I take my orders when they come in from the big boss and then we do our best to take care of our part."

Joe saw Lucy bury her face in Valentine's fur to hide her disappointment. Mr. Pink, oblivious, flagged down one of the two salespeople.

"The person in charge of the Angel Tree sure does work hard," Cami said.

Joe admired her for not giving up. She was clearly hoping to get some kind of clue as to the identity of GB, but the salesclerk was headed over and Mr. Pink was pulling on his jacket.

"Do you have any idea who's behind the Angel Tree?" Joe blurted out. It wasn't subtle but they were running out of time.

Mr. Pink shook his head. "That has to be the best-kept secret in Pine River," he said. "Jada here will help you with the hammer and I'll see you all later."

As Cami answered Jada's questions about the hammer she didn't really need, Max grabbed Joe's arm and pulled him out the door and after Mr. Pink, who was heading down the snowy sidewalk, a box of supplies tucked under one arm.

"The thing is," Max said as they caught up to the surprised store owner, "we really want to figure out who's behind the tree so we can thank them."

"We know it's supposed to be a secret," Joe said. "But it just seems to us like it's their turn to have a Christmas surprise, after all the great Christmases they've made for everyone else."

Mr. Pink nodded thoughtfully. "That's an awfully good idea," he said. "And I'd love to help. But honestly, boys, I have no idea who it is."

"Can you think of anything that might help us?" Joe asked.

Mr. Pink was quiet for a moment, considering. "Well, I'll tell you one thing I've been thinking about," he said. "It seems to me that the boss behind this whole operation is slowing down."

"Slowing down?" Max asked. "What do you mean?"

"In years past the boss got that tree up early and a wish barely lasted a day before someone was taking care of it," Mr. Pink said. The sun was setting, casting a shadow across him as he spoke. "The past few years, though, everything has taken a little longer. The tree goes up later, wishes are up longer, the instructions come slower."

"What do you think that means?" Joe asked, puzzled as to how this information fit in with what they already knew about GB.

"I suppose it could be any number of things," Mr. Pink said. "Maybe the organizer is just busier. But my guess is that the boss is getting on in years. Father Time slows us all down sooner or later, and I think he's been catching up with the boss. Now if you'll excuse me, boys, I do need to take care of this."

"Thanks," both boys called as Mr. Pink headed to his pickup truck parked across the street.

"So Mr. Pink thinks GB is getting old," Joe said, considering what this meant.

"That fits with what we know," Max said. "And the Barristers are old."

"Yeah," Joe agreed as they walked back toward the hardware store. "But it also means that we really need to find GB now more than ever."

"What do you mean?" Max asked, his eyebrows scrunching together.

"If GB is slowing down, she doesn't just need a thank-you," Joe said. "She needs help to keep the tradition of the Angel Tree alive."

Chapter 21

ᴱight Days
until Christmas

Lucy curled up on her bed with Valentine. The bingo game on Friday would be crucial, and the thought of that was a hard pit in Lucy's stomach.

She could imagine it, the bingo game, the four of them trying to stay off in the background but that being completely impossible with a blind girl clomping around after her Seeing Eye dog, especially in a new place where she was unsure about the floors being even or an unexpected throw rug. Nothing major, just enough to trip her and cause the thing they would not want: a scene. Kind of like she had made everywhere else they had gone searching for clues about GB. Just as she had suspected, except for that very first clue, Lucy had dragged things down, making them harder and slowing the search. And if she wasn't careful, it was going to happen again, Friday, the day it absolutely could not happen or it might ruin everything.

Her mother knocked on the door, making Lucy jump. "Hey, Sweetness, want to come down and set the table?" she asked.

"Sure," Lucy said, glad to have something to do besides worry.

"Dad was supposed to be home this evening, but he's not back yet," her mom said as they walked down the stairs and into the dining room. "And he didn't leave a message or anything." Her voice was thick with worry and Lucy felt a new pit in her stomach as she began laying out silverware, feeling her way around the table.

After stalling as long as they could, Lucy and her mom sat down for dinner, a serving bowl of rapidly cooling ravioli between them.

Lucy heard the click of Valentine's nails on the floor as she tried to sneak in and hide under the table to forage for any dropped food.

"Valentine, go to your bed," her mother snapped.

Lucy drew in a breath as Valentine trotted out. Yes, it annoyed her mom that Valentine liked to be under the table at meals but she never spoke to the obedient dog so sharply. Clearly her mom was really anxious about her dad.

Lucy was trying to figure out what to say when she heard the sound of the door opening and her dad's footsteps, quick and even. It was as though they'd gone back in time, to a place where her father still worked at the architecture firm and sometimes came home late, full of apologies and stories from his day.

"I'm sorry. I hope you weren't worried!" he called as he came down the hall toward the dining room.

"A bit," Lucy's mother said stiffly, in a tone that suggested she was going to have a lot more to say about this once she and Lucy's father were alone.

"I think you'll forgive me when you hear my news," her father said. Lucy felt his lips brush the top of her head in a hello kiss and then the sounds of him leaning over to kiss her mother.

"I hope it's worth our dinner getting cold," Lucy's mother said.

"Well, hm, I'm not sure," her dad said. "Lucy, would you say that your good old dad getting a new job was worth waiting for, even if it made this delicious ravioli catch a slight chill?"

Lucy shrieked and clapped her hands. Her mom jumped up, her chair scraping back as she came around the table to hug her husband.

"What's the job, Dad?" Lucy asked.

"It's with Kira Cutler's firm," her dad said. "They've been getting a lot more jobs lately and have been planning to hire a new senior architect. She was going to post the job at the start of the new year but she's been so pleased with my work on the Callahan house that she offered me the job this afternoon. We spent about an hour going over details of the contract but it's more than fair. It's a better offer than I could have hoped for and I'll start the first of the year."

"Congratulations!" Lucy said. As the news washed over her, the heaviness that had been pressing into her shoulders the past seven months was dissolving, leaving a sweet weightlessness behind.

"In a way, that's another gift we've gotten from the Angel Tree," Lucy's mom said.

"It is," her father said, beginning to serve ravioli around the table. "We've been awfully lucky this year."

As her parents discussed the details of the new job, their voices rippling with joy, Lucy felt the truth of her father's words. But it wasn't just luck. It was someone's hard work that had made this all happen. Which meant that now, more than ever, it was essential that they find GB and thank her. So if Lucy did anything at all to mess up their shot at the bingo game, she would never forgive herself.

Chapter 22

Six Days until Christmas

C ami, wait up!"

Cami's whole body stiffened at the sound of her friend Oliver's voice. She knew exactly what he was going to say and she was not looking forward to it. She turned slowly, trying to push her face into an expression of nonchalance.

"Cami, the Gala is in six days and we need you," Oliver said when he had caught up to her, concern etched across his features. "What's going on?"

"I've been really busy with school stuff." She had planned this response and hoped it came off sounding natural. "I'm struggling a little in science and, you know, school has to come first."

"Is there anything I can do?" Oliver asked. "Maybe I can help you study for the science test —"

"I'm fine," Cami said, hating how cold she sounded. But it was that or bursting into tears right there in the crowded hallway.

"Cami, come on," Max shouted from the front door of the school. "You're late!"

Normally it would have annoyed Cami to have him yell like that but now she was so relieved to escape this conversation with Oliver that she waved enthusiastically. "See you later," she said to Oliver, not able to look him in the eye. But that was a mistake because her gaze landed on the trumpet case he had cradled under one arm. It reminded her of the comforting feeling of carrying her violin. Being without it was like missing a piece of herself, and that feeling hadn't gotten any easier these past few weeks.

"Hey, Cami," Joe said, coming up beside her as she headed toward Max. He looked at her, then asked, "Are you okay?"

Cami quickly blinked back the tears that had appeared in her eyes. She couldn't fall to pieces anytime she saw someone carrying an instrument case. She was trying to be more like Willa, not become an emotional basket case. So Cami cleared her throat and grinned at Joe. "I'm great, thanks," she said.

They came to the doors of the school where Max and Lucy were waiting.

"Let's do this," Max said, his energy infectious.

The four of them headed into town, sidestepping a snowball fight at the corner of Claremont and Main Streets. They made a quick stop at Cinnamon Bakery for a bag of doughnuts, and then headed to the basement of the Pine River Baptist Church.

Cami noticed Lucy was going super slowly down the steps. "Are you hurt?" she asked her friend.

The corners of Lucy's mouth turned down. "No, just being careful," she said. Cami saw that her hands were gripping Valentine's lead so hard that her knuckles were turning white. Something was clearly going on, but before Cami could ask her, they stepped down into the crowded basement, where the bingo game was in full swing.

And now she needed to put every bit of her attention toward Mrs. Barrister. This weekend she and her grandmother were going to visit Willa and her family, and

Cami was hoping that she and her friends would have the proof they needed that the Barristers were indeed GB. She wouldn't actually tell her family the story, since she wanted to surprise them once the plans for the big thank-you celebration were in place. But just knowing they were close would make the weekend of her grandmother praising perfect Willa a lot easier to take.

As she glanced around the room filled with long tables and folding chairs for the game, she spotted her grandmother sitting next to Julia Whittaker, the two of them bent over their bingo cards. Cami couldn't help smiling a bit; her grandmother was very serious about her bingo.

"Mrs. Barrister is over there," Max said in an exaggerated whisper as they stood at the foot of the stairs, taking in the scene.

"I don't think she can hear you this far away," Cami said in her normal voice. Mrs. Barrister was at a table at the opposite side of the large, drafty room, hunched over her bingo cards. Cami's heart clenched up as she thought about the fact that Mrs. Barrister had lost her son. Her white hair was falling out of its bun in wisps and her blue cardigan hung off her thin body like a cape.

Max raised any eyebrow. "You can never be too careful. I think we should come up with a few hand gestures before we get closer."

Cami and Joe snickered, though Lucy didn't seem to have even heard. "Why would we need to communicate silently?" Cami asked.

"Who knows if we might need to act quickly," Max said.

"What, in case she makes a break for it?" Cami asked. "I don't think she'll be moving very fast." She gestured toward the walker next to Mrs. Barrister.

Before Max could respond, a shout of *Bingo* came from the front row.

"I won!" Cami's neighbor Wilbur Jenkins called out.

Mrs. Whipple, who was famous for chasing kids off her lawn with an umbrella, whipped her head around. "Better check that card," she yelled. "He's a known cheater."

Cami cringed at the words as she watched kind Mr. Jenkins, who always cleared their driveway and front path with his snowblower after storms, sag a bit in his seat.

Right in front of them, Clara Mitchell, the town registrar, stood up. "Hogwash," she called out indignantly.

"Mrs. Whipple, I'm quite sure I remember the only cheater we've ever had at this game was you, last month."

Mrs. Whipple sent a stinging glare at Mrs. Mitchell, who held her pose defiantly.

Cami was torn between being appalled at how they were acting and wanting to laugh.

"Let's break for some coffee," Mrs. Johnson said, running a hand through her salt-and-pepper hair. Cami noted that she looked tired.

"This is our chance," Max whispered, starting toward the refreshment table set up at the back of the room. The bingo players were slowly standing up and heading over.

Cami trailed behind Max as he walked up to Mrs. Barrister, who was carefully taking a Nutter Butter from a tray of cookies.

"Good afternoon, Mrs. Barrister," he said.

Her hand froze and she looked up nervously. "Do I know you?" she asked.

"I am a youth at the local school right here in Pine River," Max said.

Cami stifled a laugh at his formal declaration but Mrs. Barrister continued to look at him uneasily.

"Do you have any plans for Christmas?" Max asked.

Mrs. Barrister looked alarmed, as though she worried Max might invite himself over for Christmas dinner. "Just a quiet evening at home," she said.

"That sounds great," Max said.

Cami could hear the edge of desperation in his voice and she wracked her brain for a way she might be able to help. "Christmas is such a special time of year," she said. "And there are so many wonderful Christmas traditions here in Pine River." It was lame but Max shot her a grateful look.

"Yes, like the Angel Tree," he said.

Mrs. Barrister pressed a hand to her forehead as though the conversation was too much for her. "The what?"

Cami was getting a sinking feeling in her chest.

"The Angel Tree?" Max said. "Where people hang up wishes and other people help them come true."

Mrs. Barrister's brow wrinkled in genuine confusion. "I'm not aware of that," she said.

Max's shoulders drooped. "Enjoy the cookies," he said.

Mrs. Barrister gave him an odd look but Max was already walking away, Cami and the others behind him.

The weight of their failure was pressing down on Cami's chest but she bit her lip, wanting to keep it together while they were still surrounded by half the town.

Joe was shaking his head. "I can't believe she's lived here all this time and doesn't know about the Angel Tree. Even I know about it."

"It is weird," Max said. "I guess they really do like to keep to themselves."

"I think it's the grief," Joe said. There was a faraway look in his eyes and Cami knew he was thinking about his mom. She reached over and squeezed his arm.

"We should do something to help them," Max said.

"Yes, let's," Lucy said. Cami saw that her face and hands had relaxed, which Cami didn't fully understand because now she herself was barely able to hold back tears.

"Cami, darling, introduce me to your friends," her grandmother called. She was standing with Mr. Jenkins, a paper cup of coffee in one hand, and the four of them headed over.

After she had shaken Lucy's and Joe's hands, Cami's grandmother gave Cami a quizzical look. "What were you talking to Mrs. Barrister about?" she asked.

And that's when Cami realized she could at least do one thing right today. She could tell her grandmother about the Barristers, because sure Willa could be helpful, but Cami's grandmother? When she put her mind to helping someone, it was like Wonder Woman had taken over the job.

Cami told her grandmother and Mr. Jenkins what the boys had seen at the Barristers' home, with Joe adding details.

"Oh, those poor people," Cami's grandmother said sympathetically. "And to think they've just shut themselves off from everyone, carrying all that grief alone." She straightened her shoulders. "We'll have to take care of that right now. I'm going to ask Mrs. Barrister to join our knitting circle and I'm not going to take no for an answer."

"I can ask Mr. Barrister to join the men's Bible group," Mr. Jenkins said, his eyes lighting up.

"And we'll be sure to take them with us to the Christmas Gala," Cami's grandmother said in a determined voice. She started to walk toward Mrs. Barrister, then turned back to Cami and her friends. "You kids did a good thing telling us," she said. "And we're going to take it from here."

Cami grinned, knowing that the Barristers were in very good hands and feeling pleased that she had done something her grandmother was proud of. But even though it was something good, it wasn't close to something Willa would do. Something like finding and thanking GB. So as she followed her friends back up the stairs and out into the chilly afternoon, the fact that they had failed to find GB came crashing back down on her. And Cami did the only thing she could: She burst into tears.

Chapter 23

Six Days
until Christmas

J oe froze, shocked at the sight of Cami, the one who always kept them going, looking so defeated.

"Cami, it's going to be okay," Lucy said, struggling forward to hug Cami.

"We're going to find GB," Max said grimly.

Joe finally found his voice. "Yeah, we are," he said. "We're going to get a whole new list of suspects — I mean, possibilities — and we won't stop till we know who GB is." As he spoke he realized he wasn't just comforting Cami; this was what he wanted, too, more than anything.

"But we only have six days till Christmas," Cami said. Her voice was shaky but Joe was relieved to see that the tears had stopped. "And I'm away this weekend."

"It doesn't matter," Max said determinedly. "We'll all brainstorm this weekend and then when we meet on Monday we'll be ready to go."

"And you think we'll find GB?" Cami asked.

"I know it," Max said.

"Me too," Joe agreed.

Lucy gave a small smile. "Me three."

Cami took a deep breath. "Okay, then," she said, wiping the last of the tears off her face. "We'll get this done."

An icy wind whipped around the buildings in the town square and the branches of the Angel Tree, now with most of the wishes plucked, danced in the gusts. Joe burrowed into his warm jacket, thankful to not be freezing.

"Where are you going this weekend, Cami?" he asked as they began walking. He knew the others were probably eager to get home but he wasn't. Leon was away on business until the next day and Joe was dreading the night by himself in the dark apartment.

"My aunt's house," Cami said, wrinkling her nose. "I'll get to hear how great my cousin is all weekend. What are you guys doing?" She was looking and sounding like herself again, which was a relief.

"We're going out to dinner to celebrate my dad's new job," Lucy said. She had told them the good news about her dad's job over lunch.

Cami glanced at Joe expectantly, but he had nothing to say. Something jagged rattled in his chest as he pictured the long weekend alone.

"Joe's coming over to my house," Max said.

Joe jerked his head back in surprise. "What?" he asked.

"You're camping out at my place this weekend," Max said like it had already been decided.

Joe wanted to say yes so much it hurt and that scared him. He'd gone for months without letting himself need anything, closing himself off from people and this town. The thought of opening himself back up now seemed dangerous, like a bad idea he needed to back away from. "I'm not sure —" he began.

But Max cut him off. "My little sister's having a slumber party and I'll be drowning in American Girls and My Little Pony. You've got to help me out."

"Go," Cami said. "Max needs you."

"My Little Pony can be *really* scary," Lucy said, and she and Cami cracked up.

Max laughed too, but Joe, weighed down by the decision, couldn't even smile.

"Joe, I've been meaning to ask you, when is your mom coming?" Cami asked, serious again. "I really want to meet her. I've never met a real live soldier before."

Lucy was nodding. "I want to meet her too. Maybe you guys can all come over to dinner one night while she's here. My dad makes amazing spaghetti and meatballs."

It had already happened, Joe realized as Max began talking about the chocolate cake his mom would bake for the dinner. Somehow in the past weeks this group of three people had nestled themselves into the place Joe had thought he'd shut away. They'd been there for him, they'd helped him, and they'd taken the help he offered. There was no deciding now what they meant to him: It had already been decided. They were his friends, plain and simple. All he had to do now was say yes.

"A dinner would be great," he said. "My mom will love it. And, Max, I'll protect you from the evil that is My Little Pony."

As Joe headed back with Max across the square, he looked up at the Angel Tree, a dark silhouette against the blue-black sky. He thought about everything the tree had given to him: the visit from his mom; the friendships with Max, Cami, and Lucy; and something even deeper than that too.

Pine River had become his home.

Chapter 24

Six Days until Christmas

Max kicked back on his bed as Joe looked around his room. Well, his temporary room. But knowing that one day his family would be in their new house made living in the temporary apartment a whole lot easier.

"You have all the Harry Potter books," Joe said, leaning over Max's bookcase. "I love those!"

"Me too," Max said. "Though it took me forever to get through them. I kind of suck at reading." The words just slipped out. Max almost never talked about his school struggles, even with Cami. He tensed up, waiting for Joe to make a joke about it.

But Joe had moved on to Max's DVD collection and

didn't seem to care. "I cheated and watched the movies first," he said. "Though I liked the books better."

Max leaned back against his pillows. "Want to watch one of those?" he asked, gesturing to the box of DVDs. Max had an old TV in his room that didn't have cable but was hooked up to their ancient DVD player.

"Yeah," Joe said.

Max stood up. "Let's make some popcorn to eat while we watch."

"How can you even think of eating after that dinner we just ate?" Joe asked, slapping a hand on his stomach.

Max's mom had made her famous mac and cheese for Max's sister's slumber party. While the girls had taken their plates into the living room to eat in front of an American Girl movie, Max had watched in awe as Joe devoured four servings of the creamy mac. Later they'd all had ice cream with caramel sauce and Christmassy red and green M&M's on top. Max had been pretty full but the meal had been over an hour ago and he was ready to eat again, especially something like popcorn, which was practically eating air. "More for me if you don't want any," Max said.

He expected Joe to respond but Joe was looking intently at a book in his hand.

"You're into karate?" Max asked, glancing at the title as he stood up. He hoped there was some Parmesan to sprinkle on the popcorn.

"No, I just, I never said sorry," Joe said, his cheeks suddenly flushed.

"For not doing karate?" Max was confused.

"For punching you that day," Joe said, putting the book down but not quite looking at Max. "It was a jerky thing to do and I'm sorry."

Max hadn't even thought about the punch in what felt like ages. But the fact that Joe had thought about it and apologized — that meant something to Max. Though of course he wasn't going to say that. "No big deal," he said. "But now that I think of it, you do kind of owe me."

Joe laughed and put down the book. "I think not," he said. "What movie are we watching?"

"How about *The Deathly Hallows Part 1*?" Max asked. "But let's get the popcorn first."

Max opened the door of his bedroom and the boys walked down the hall. The girls were spread out in sleeping bags across the small living room, passing bowls of chips and pretzels as they watched a movie with a lot of girls wearing pink. The chips looked irresistible, so he snuck a bowl from the table, and headed to the kitchen for sodas.

"I think I already have a headache coming on," his dad said as the girls in the living room all began shrieking. "They seem to do that every ten minutes or so."

"What are they screaming about?" Joe asked.

Max's dad shook his head. "Girls are a mystery, Joe," he said. "Who knows why they do anything?"

"It's you boys who are the mystery," Max's mom said, coming up behind him. Her long hair was coming out of its ponytail. "Why you feel compelled to leave your socks on the living room floor every night is the biggest mystery out there."

Max passed Joe the chips and headed out, sodas in hand, leaving his parents to have the sock conversation for the millionth time.

Once they were back in his room, he began flipping through his DVDs to find *The Deathly Hallows*.

"Your family's really nice," Joe said.

Normally Max would have made a joke about them but, glancing at Joe, he didn't feel like he needed to. "Yeah, they're pretty cool," he said.

When the movie was loaded, they settled on the floor, bowl of chips between them. As the opening credits began, Max's mind was only half on the screen. He was thinking about how easy it was to be with Joe, how comfortable it was to just say whatever he wanted without worrying about being the funniest guy in the room or the next prank he was going to pull.

Over the music of the movie, Max heard another round of shrieking start up in the living room. Joe pretended to cover his ears, and Max laughed.

Max wasn't sure if they would ever find GB, but he did know this: He owed GB the biggest, best thank-you ever. Because this year, thanks to the Angel Tree, Max had a new home on its way, a new friend, and the freedom to make a choice. For a while Max had been getting tired of being the class clown. But it was only now that he'd made a new friend just by being himself that he could imagine retiring from his life of pranking. Of course, he would still pull off the occasional stunt; skills like this could not be contained forever.

But after years of being the funny guy, Max was ready to just be Max.

———✳———

Chapter 25

Four Days until Christmas

T he snow was coming down in thick, wet flakes as Cami made her way through town to the square. It was dinnertime on a Sunday, so the square was pretty deserted and the stores on Main Street were mostly dark. But the Angel Tree was there, lights shining through a fresh layer of snow, as Cami hung her wish. The branches swayed gently in the wind and for a moment it looked like Cami's wish might take flight.

Cami knew it was too late for her real wish, the wish to get her own violin back. And it was probably too late for this one too. But it had felt like the only thing to do and so she was here, in the middle of a near blizzard, trying to fix the mistake she had made almost a month earlier.

The weekend at her aunt's had been awful. Everyone was all worked up about some math camp Willa had been accepted to. And whenever they had stopped crowing about that, they had talked in rapturous voices about the important work she was doing at the hospital. Cami and the other cousins had been swept to the side, mere shadows in the face of Willa's bright light. The worst had been watching her grandmother fawn all over Willa like she was the favorite granddaughter, with Cami a distant second at best. And not a single person asked Cami about her violin.

Between the awful weekend and the failure to find GB, Cami was officially giving up. She would never be as good as Willa. She had tried and she'd failed. There was only one thing she was really good at and she had stupidly tossed it aside. She had sold the one thing that was really, truly her.

Which was why she was here. Her violin was gone but maybe someone in town would take pity on her and buy her another, or work out a rental with Palomino Music. Before, Cami had been a snob about the quality of the violin, appreciating that hers was top-notch. But now she would play anything; she was like a starving person, desperate to play music any way she could.

As she headed back home, the snow falling softly on her cheeks, Cami realized that she was asking for more than a violin. She was asking for her heart back.

That night after dinner, as Cami and her grandmother were washing up, the doorbell rang.

"My land," Cami's grandmother said. "Who could it be at this hour?"

"I'll get it," Cami said, drying her hands on a dish towel before hurrying to open the door.

There, on the snowy front stoop, stood Mr. Carmichael, the conductor of the school orchestra, his black peacoat studded with melting snowflakes.

"Hello, Cami," he said in his velvety voice. "I haven't seen you at orchestra rehearsals, so I wanted to stop by and see how the solo is coming along."

Cami stood stricken and silent in the doorway, her mind whirling in panic as she fought for some kind of rational response. How could she possibly admit what

DAPHNE BENEDIS-GRAB

she had done? And why hadn't she thought to tell him that he would need to find another soloist? This was a disaster.

"Cami, don't leave Mr. Carmichael out in the cold," her grandmother scolded gently from behind her.

Cami managed to step aside so Mr. Carmichael could come in, but she did not release her grip on the door — she needed to hold on to that or she might collapse.

"I came to check in with Cami about her solo for the Gala," Mr. Carmichael said. "I wanted to be sure she's feeling prepared."

"How thoughtful of you," Cami heard her grandmother say. "I'm sure she'll be set for the concert with just a bit more practice."

Cami could not bear to turn around and face what was going to have to happen.

"Sweetie, close the door and go upstairs and practice your solo," her grandmother said. She was using her polite-for-company voice but Cami heard the order underneath the softness.

Cami swallowed and shut the door slowly, then turned, her eyes down.

"Darling, take your violin and go upstairs to practice," her grandmother said.

There was no avoiding it: Cami had to tell her the truth. She raised her eyes and then she froze, her mind coming to a grinding halt.

Her grandmother was holding a violin, *her* violin, in her arms.

"Take it, darling," her grandmother said gently.

So Cami did, a rush of tears coming into her eyes as her hands closed over the case.

"And now go play," her grandmother said.

Cami flew up the stairs clutching her violin close. Up in her room, she opened the case and feasted her eyes on her beloved violin, the softly curved wood feeling perfect in her hands as she picked it up. She tuned it lovingly, then lifted it and tucked it securely under her chin.

There were tears on her cheeks as she began to play, but Cami didn't notice. She was unaware of anything but the music pouring through her.

Hours later, Cami headed downstairs for a snack, her feet light and her heart soaring as she headed into the kitchen. Her grandmother stood at the stove, heating water for her tea.

It was only then that the questions came to Cami. "How did you know about my violin?" she asked.

Her grandmother turned with a raised eyebrow. "Did you honestly believe Ms. Tennyson would let a twelve-year-old girl sell her most precious possession?"

Cami was confused. "But she told me she sold it."

"Well, I suppose in a matter of speaking she did," her grandmother said, taking out her box of peppermint tea. "As soon as you left the store, she called me and asked what I wanted her to do."

"What did you say?" Cami asked, pulling out a chair and sitting down at their small kitchen table.

"I asked her to sell it to me," her grandmother replied. "Which she only agreed to do because I insisted she tell you that the violin had sold. And of course then she gave all the money I'd given her to you. I hope you spent it well."

"Yes," Cami said, thinking of the gifts for her grandmother tucked under her bed. "But why did you want me to think it had sold?"

Her grandmother turned and looked at Cami through the steam rising from her teacup. "Because you wanted to sell it," she said simply. "It seemed obvious to me that you were working something out. I figured I'd hold on to your violin until you realized how much you needed it."

Cami cocked her head. "How did you know to give it to me tonight?"

Her grandmother grinned as she sat down across from Cami. "I think Mr. Carmichael had spies on the Angel Tree twenty-four hours a day. He was in quite a tizzy about you and that solo. But I told him you'd come around before Christmas."

That all this had been happening without her having the slightest hint was astounding to Cami.

"So did you?" her grandmother asked.

"Did I what?" Cami asked.

"Work out what needed working," her grandmother said. "Because for you to have given up that violin, I'm thinking it must have been something pretty big."

Cami looked down at the table. "I wanted to be more like Willa," she said softly. "And do things that help people so you would be proud of me."

Her grandmother was silent. When Cami finally screwed up the courage to look at her, she saw that her grandmother was slowly shaking her head. "Darling, how could you, for one second, not know how incredibly proud I am of you and that beautiful music you make?"

"It's just, you were telling Aunt Aisha how great Willa was and how you wished I was more like her," Cami said, rubbing her finger along the edge of the wooden table.

Her grandmother reached over and smoothed back a braid that had fallen over Cami's face. "Willa's having a hard time right now," she said. "She's been the target of some pretty mean-spirited bullying at school. Everyone in the family has been working to lift her back up. And her parents too. They feel like they failed her and so we're all rallying around, trying to give them back what's been taken in all this."

Everything was shifting in Cami's mind as she took in her grandmother's words.

"But it seems I took something from you," her grandmother went on. "And that I never meant to do. Not when I'm so proud of you and your talents and your good heart." She reached out and set her hand gently on top of

THE ANGEL TREE

Cami's. "You *do* help people. Your music brings everyone who hears it pure joy, a moment away from their lives where they can feel at peace. And Lord knows we all need that. Hearing you play is a gift, and I've been thankful for it since you first picked up that violin."

Cami jumped up from the table and threw her arms around her grandmother, almost knocking over her tea.

But her grandmother just laughed and held Cami close, her soft cheek pressing against Cami's. "You just wait till you get an earful of all that boasting I'll be doing at the Gala," she murmured in Cami's ear.

Cami let go of her grandmother. "I should have told you what I was planning to do before I sold my violin," she said. "I'm sorry."

But her grandmother waved her apology away. "Sometimes we need to live something before we know it," she said. "I'm guessing you found out some pretty important truths these past few weeks."

"I did," Cami said, feeling the certainty of this.

"Then it was a journey well taken," her grandmother said.

That night, in the moonlight shining through her bed-room window, Cami could see her violin on the chair next to the music stand. Knowing that it was right where it belonged, and that her grandmother felt the same way, made Cami's heart sing.

Chapter 26

✴

Three Days until Christmas

S o I hear I have your helping hands this afternoon," Ms. Marwich said as Max walked into the library during his one free period of the day.

"Yeah," Max said glumly. Last week Max had gotten caught with a small can of shaving cream in the computer lab and now he was stuck with a makeup detention. He swore to himself that it would be his last.

"Well, I'm thrilled to have the assistance," Ms. Marwich said, as though Max had chosen to come. Still, she looked like she meant it, which lifted his spirits a bit.

"What do you need me to do?" he asked.

"Let's get you started with shelving," Ms. Marwich said, walking him over to a big cart of books. "I've had so many returns lately that I've fallen behind. It'll be great to get these back where they belong. You remember the system?"

Max nodded. This was not his first detention in the library. "I'm on it," he said.

Max wheeled the cart to the nonfiction section of the library and picked up the first book. *The Mysteries of the Digestive System Revealed.* Who checked out a book like that? Maybe it was for a science paper. Still, when Max flipped through the book and saw a diagram of the digestive system, with its slimy coils of intestines, he was thoroughly grossed out. Some things were definitely better left mysteries.

The library was quiet; the only sound was the clicking of Ms. Marwich's fingers on her computer keyboard and the occasional clank from the radiator. The smell of lemon cleanser and books was somehow soothing, especially given the cozy warmth of the room, and soon Max was lulled into a routine, barely even noticing the names on the books as he checked numbers and shelved. Until he came to a familiar title: *Create the Dress, Create Yourself.* That had been the title of the book on the dress patterns Olivia Potter had gotten from her Angel Tree wish. It was just strange enough that it had stuck in Max's mind.

Max checked the number on the spine and put the book in the craft section, all the while thinking about what this might mean. Possibly nothing but possibly — Max knelt in front of the cart of books, scanning the titles. On the second row he saw one that set off bells: *Pastries and Cakes from Around the World.* He pulled it off and turned to the table of contents. Sure enough, there was a section on Russian pastries, exactly what Lana Levkov had wished for at the Angel Tree.

Max was fired up as he started shelving books again, his mind only partially on the task in front of him. He didn't want to jump to conclusions, a problem that had brought down many a spy in some of his favorite movies, but the evidence seemed convincing. Whoever had fulfilled these wishes, and possibly others he didn't know about, had done so using the school library.

Max began looking at titles as he shelved, thinking about how others, like *Home Makeovers* or *Computer Programming Made Easy* might have been used to make a wish come true. He hoped the gross digestion book and another he picked up about hang gliding weren't involved in wishes, but others definitely had the potential to be. Which, Max decided, could mean one of two things: A lot of people just happened to use the school library when they plucked wishes from the Angel Tree. Or, GB used the school library as one of her resources for coordinating all the wishes from the tree.

It seemed unlikely that a whole slew of people stopped by the school library for help with wishes. Most of the people who took the white scraps of paper were adults who were far more likely to use the public library right in the town square. Which left the other possibility: GB was using the school library. And the only reason she would do that, Max reasoned, would be if she had some kind of connection to the school.

"How's it going?"

Max jumped.

"I didn't mean to scare you," the librarian said. "You certainly are focused."

"Yeah, I just want to be sure to get everything in the right place," Max said, embarrassed by his reaction.

"I'm sure you're doing just fine," Ms. Marwich said, patting him on the shoulder. "You're nearly done and I can finish up these last few. You've given me the help

I needed to be able to go home a bit early for my book club."

"You do more reading outside this?" Max asked, gesturing at the room filled with books.

Ms. Marwich laughed. "I actually don't get to read during the day, though you'd think I would! I'm too busy helping other people pick out books. So I'm in a classics book club to read the great authors and then I'm also in a mystery reading club. That's the one meeting today."

"Sounds fun," Max said, though honestly he couldn't imagine wanting to spend all that time reading and talking about books.

Ms. Marwich was smiling as though she could read his mind, which she probably could. "I enjoy it," she said.

It occurred to Max that she might know who had borrowed some of the books he'd been shelving. "I was wondering, actually," he said, "if you know who took out some of the books I shelved. Like there was one called *Create the Dress, Create Yourself.* And another about pastries."

Ms. Marwich seemed surprised at the question. She looked at Max intently. "Is there a reason you're asking?"

Max felt squirmy under her gaze. "No, I was just curious," he said.

"Okay," she said, her eyes still on Max's face. "But I'm sorry, I don't like to give out information like that. The librarian-reader relationship is confidential, at least in my book."

"No problem," Max said.

Ms. Marwich smiled at him, the intensity gone. Or maybe Max had just imagined it in the first place. "Go ahead and take the last few minutes to relax."

"Thanks," Max said. He headed out of the library, his mind on the meeting he would be having with Cami, Joe, and Lucy that afternoon and how this latest clue might help them.

Chapter 27

———— ✳ ————

Three Days
until Christmas

H ey, Lucy," Anya called as Lucy closed up her
locker. "Want to come over this afternoon?"

Lucy did want to — it had been a while
since she'd been to Anya's. But she'd agreed to meet
Cami, Joe, and Max in the library and she didn't want
to break her promise. "I can't today but what about
tomorrow?"

"Sure," Anya said. "See you later."

Lucy's spirits were low as she trudged into the library
for the meeting. They had planned to talk at lunch but
instead ended up reliving Cami's story about her violin.
Lucy loved hearing her friend's voice bubble over with
joy, but a piece of her had shriveled as Cami spoke. For

weeks Cami had dropped hints that she was unhappy, that there was something worrying her, but Lucy had never taken the time to follow up. She had been a bad friend to Cami and that hung heavy on her, just like their failure to find GB was a weight pressing down on her chest. And it wasn't like she'd really sabotaged anything but she couldn't help wondering if things had moved faster, which they would have if Lucy hadn't been slowing them, they would have ruled out everyone on their list faster and had more time to track down the real GB. Now, with three days till Christmas, they had precious little time to track down GB and plan a really amazing celebration.

As she and Valentine walked into the large library, Lucy heard the librarian say, "Here," and then slide something across a table.

"Oh, she's darling," Ms. Ortega, the art teacher, cooed.

"Isn't she adorable?" Ms. Marwich said. "She's my brother's first grandchild. Everyone in the family is simply — oh, hello, Lucy and Valentine."

"Hi," Lucy said as they came up to the desk, Valentine leading Lucy carefully around Ms. Ortega.

"Your friends await," Ms. Marwich said.

"Thanks," Lucy said, heading back.

"So what's her name?" Ms. Ortega asked after Lucy had passed.

"Elizabeth Berle," Ms. Marwich said.

Something about that made Lucy pause but before she could figure out exactly what, Cami was ushering her in. Lucy sat down and Valentine settled at her feet with a sigh.

"Lucy's here, so let's get started," Cami said. She was serious but Lucy could still hear the happiness in her voice. "We have only three days until Christmas and we still need to *find* GB and then plan something really spectacular. So that means we need to get cracking."

"I have some new intel," Max said, and he recounted his discovery in the library.

"Can anyone take out books here or just people at the school?" Joe asked.

"I'm not sure," Cami said. "Though I don't know why anyone else would want to use the school library when there's a perfectly good public library right on Main Street."

"Right, that's what I was thinking," Max said. "It has to mean that there's a tie between GB and the school."

"I bet GB's a teacher!" Cami exclaimed.

"Or it could be someone with a kid who goes here," Joe added.

"Let's start our new list of suspects," Max said. Lucy could hear him rubbing his palms together eagerly.

"How many times have I told you, there are no suspects?" Cami asked playfully.

"Okay, possible Great Benefactors," Max said in an exaggerated English accent.

They were still no closer to finding GB, but everyone seemed happy anyway. Everyone except Lucy.

"What about Kira Cutler?" Max asked. "She's the one designing the plans for my new house, so we know she's generous. And her son is in eighth grade, so she has a connection to the school."

Lucy poked a finger through a small hole in her sweater sleeve as her friends went on. She didn't have anything to offer and she didn't feel like getting involved in the discussion.

"Lucy, what do you think?" Cami asked, picking up on Lucy's distance from the conversation.

Lucy shrugged. "I don't know," she said.

"Does anyone know if Kira's a big reader?" Joe asked,

freeing Lucy to go back to her thoughts. Which seemed to be just brooding.

"I bet we can find out," Cami said. "Oh, but her last name doesn't start with B."

B. Berle. Ms. Marwich's brother's last name. Which would make it Ms. Marwich's family name. And Lucy knew Ms. Marwich's first name was Rona. An R. As in . . . RB. Lucy's heart began to race. "You guys . . ." she began.

She spoke softly but Cami must have seen something in her face because she immediately hushed the boys.

"I think . . . I just figured out GB," Lucy said. "It's Ms. Marwich." Max started to chime in but Lucy raised her hand to stop him. "Just hear me out. First of all there's how she smells," Lucy said, thinking it through as she spoke.

"What?" Max asked incredulously.

Cami laughed. "Lucy has an amazing sense of smell," she said. "She always knows it's me because of my bubble-gum lip gloss."

"What do I smell like?" Max asked.

"No one wants to get into that," Cami said impatiently. "Let Lucy speak."

"Ms. Marwich has this lilac lotion but recently she's smelled like other things too," Lucy continued, things clicking into place as she spoke. "Like a while ago she smelled like the vet's office. I thought she'd brought her cat in, but she'd said Tango was fine. So maybe she helped with Valentine's surgery, setting it up and then going in to pay after we had our last appointment. And a few weeks ago she smelled like lavender — like the Hobby Horse, where she probably got Olivia's sewing machine."

"That's pretty cool," Joe said admiringly. "Like a super power or something."

"Yeah," Max agreed. "Though I'm not sure Smell Girl is going to work as a name."

"What about —" Joe began, but Lucy cut him off, excited.

"Also, she's a book lover and she's obviously connected to the library."

Max drew in a breath. "Wait a second," he said. "When I asked Ms. Marwich about those books, the ones we think GB got out of the library, she was weird about it. I figured I was just imagining it but now I'm not so sure."

"Weird how?" Cami asked.

"Just really serious, asking me why I wanted to know," Max said. "And she also told me she's in like twenty book clubs, so she's a major reader."

Lucy was about to reply when Joe spoke up.

"I don't think Ms. Marwich is rich," he said. "And that was one of the traits on the list."

"Maybe we were wrong about that one," Cami said thoughtfully. "Maybe you don't need that much money to be GB, just a lot of good helpers."

Lucy heard a shift in the way her friends were breathing as an intensity began to build in the room as the pieces came together, and her own pulse was racing.

"We know she's really generous," Max said. "So that part fits too. But are these things really enough to prove she's GB?"

"There's one more thing," Lucy said. "And it's the most important. Just now I heard her say that Berle was her family name. Rona Berle. Just like the RB on the bookmark. That's all our clues and she fits every one."

"Lucy," Cami said, her voice tinged with awe. "You did it. You figured out GB."

She had. As her friends began crowing at their victory, and suggesting plans for the celebration, Lucy sat quietly, letting it sink in. This whole time she had thought her blindness was making everything harder when in fact, she had been able to see what the rest of them had not. She had been the one to put together the delicate trail of clues and now they were going to be able to thank GB — Ms. Marwich — for the incredible gifts she had given to the town.

"And you thought you were holding us back," Cami said, patting Lucy's arm. "We'd never have figured it out without you."

"You're the best spy among us," Max added.

"We're not spies," Cami said.

"Well, you're not, obviously," Max said. "I mean, you were convinced GB was the VonWolfs."

Lucy couldn't help laughing at that, then the sound of Cami smacking Max's arm and Max's howl of protest.

"We should get going," Joe said. "We can't plan a party for Ms. Marwich when she's right out there."

"Come over for dinner," Cami said. "We can plan at my place. My grandma can help."

Everyone agreed and then they headed out, all trying to sound casual as they came up to Ms. Marwich.

"Leaving already?" she asked.

"Yes," Cami said, her voice high and totally un-Cami-like, which made Lucy, who was already amped up, burst into giggles.

"They're just excited about our mission," Max said, trying to help.

"What mission is that?" Ms. Marwich asked pleasantly.

Lucy suddenly worried they were on the verge of giving everything away but luckily Joe kept his head. "Sorry, that's top secret," he said. "And we should get going. Bye, Ms. Marwich!"

The four of them hustled out of the library.

"I can't believe it's her," Cami said as they walked down the hall. "But at the same time it makes perfect sense. She's one of the most generous people I've ever met."

"She was the first person who talked to me when I moved here," Joe said.

"And she never made me feel like an idiot all those times I had detention with her," Max said.

"She always says hi to Valentine," Lucy said. "She really is awesome."

"We are going to give her the best Christmas celebration ever," Cami said. "To thank her for everything she's done for us and everyone else in town."

"I'm game," Max said. Lucy heard the slippery sound of him sliding his arms into his coat as they neared the front door of the school.

"Same," Joe said.

For a moment Lucy felt the tug of resistance, the fear that she would hinder more than she helped. But then she remembered — she had been the one to figure out GB. "I'm in too," she said.

And the joy in her voice mirrored that of her friends. Because thanks to the Angel Tree, Lucy had her beloved dog, her new friends, and, most of all, the knowledge that she was capable of just about anything.

And that was a gift that would last forever.

Chapter 28

Christmas Day

The last note of Cami Patrick's solo shimmered in the starry night and for a moment Ms. Marwich and the crowd gathered in the Pine River town square for the Christmas Gala stood in perfect silence, the beauty of the music washing over them. Then the applause broke out, thunderous and strong as Cami took a quick bow.

"Thank you for coming and a very Merry Christmas to all!" Mr. Carmichael called out, officially ending the Christmas Gala.

As always Ms. Marwich had enjoyed every moment, from the toddler sing-along to the gorgeous solo Cami Patrick had played. She searched for Cami when the musicians came down from the stage but, after looking for a good ten minutes, was unable to locate her. Perhaps she and her grandmother had rushed off to prepare for their Chistmas dinner. Ms. Marwich had nothing to rush home to, so she stayed, chatting with friends and neighbors and drinking the hot cider being served in front of the makeshift stage. Everyone was discussing how this year's Gala had been the best ever. It was a comment Ms. Marwich had heard for the past thirty years and each year it was true.

As she walked to get a second cup of cider, she was pleasantly surprised to see the Barristers each holding paper cups of cider, looking shy but happy to be part of things. She stopped to greet them, then to say hi to Alma Sanchez. One by one families drifted off toward home to eat their Christmas dinner together. Ms. Marwich remained as the square slowly emptied, stirring her cooling cider with a cinnamon stick and talking with several town library board members. But she knew it was time to finally head home when they once again invited her to join the board in the coming year. It was an invitation she had turned down many times, each time feeling guilty but always knowing that it was a commitment she simply could not afford to make. Not when she needed every spare moment she had for the Angel Tree.

She had started the Angel Tree the year her husband had died in a car accident. They had no children and with the loss of her husband, Ms. Marwich's life had been ripped apart, a gaping hole at its center. She had only lived in Pine River for five years but the townsfolk rallied around her, organizing neighbors to bring her dinner each night, mowing her lawn, then raking her leaves, and finally plowing her front path and driveway. As winter settled in and the looming prospect of her first Christmas alone approached, she had taken stock of things. She decided that rather than mourn what she didn't have, she would do something for the town that had helped her heal. She could never get her husband back but she could help other people get what they needed, the wishes closest to their hearts. And so the Angel Tree began.

That first year had started small but she'd seen children get supplies they needed to pursue their passions, adults get the one thing they needed to survive a rough patch, and the kindness of neighbors as the people of Pine River gave most of the gifts that adorned the tree.

When it was done and Christmas arrived, Ms. Marwich had felt a sense of joy she had not believed could be possible after her loss. And so every year she made the arrangements to put up the tree, helped organize the wishes that were complicated, and fulfilled those that were left. Every year it brought her rich contentment to see the people of Pine River, who had been there for her, come together and support each other.

But as she headed home in the frosty night air, sadness tinged the elation she felt for this year's tree. Because now, with her bank account dwindling and her aging body aching from the toll of all the work, Ms. Marwich was not sure she could do it another year. She sighed, pushing the thought away. There would be time to consider what could be done next week. Right now all she wanted was to get home to her quiet little house and climb into bed.

Snow began to fall as she turned onto her block, gentle flakes that glowed in the lights and decorations carefully set up in each yard and on each house. Except, of course, for her own house at the end of the street. December was always such a whirlwind of activities for the Angel Tree that it left her no time to decorate her home or prepare any kind of Christmas feast. In fact, this year she had not even managed to go grocery shopping in the days leading up to the holiday. She would be eating leftovers if she could muster up the energy to heat them.

She was shivering a bit as she passed the Murrays' home. The bushes in their yard were covered with twinkling colored lights that matched the lights strung along the roof of their home. A lit candle glowed in each window and a carefully woven wreath hung on their door. Ms. Marwich took a moment to admire it before walking on to her house, which she knew would be dark.

Except that it wasn't. Ms. Marwich stopped on the sidewalk and blinked, wondering if her fatigue was causing some kind of vision problem. But as she looked again, the truth was undeniable. Her home was adorned with lights, the bushes in her yard decorated with delicate poinsettia blossoms, and on her door hung a wreath dotted with bright red holly berries. Her windows were lit up and each had a candle casting its soft light out into the black night. It was a thing of beauty and Ms. Marwich's breath caught in her throat as she drank it in.

But then curiosity overtook her. Who had sneaked into her home and created such a delightful surprise? She hurried up the freshly shoveled stone path to her front door to find out.

The first thing she noticed when she pushed open the heavy door was the swirl of delicious smells that greeted her: If the fragrance was anything to go by, a true feast had been prepared while she was away.

Ms. Marwich hurried down the hall to the open living and dining room and then she gasped, a hand flying to her chest. Colored Christmas lights had been strung along the walls, bathing the room in a festive glow. The big wooden table was laden with scrumptious food — crackling duck, fluffy biscuits, fresh baked apple pie. And crowded around it was what seemed like the entire town of Pine River. Dozens of people were crammed into the room, with more spilling into the kitchen and onto the back deck.

"Surprise!" everyone shouted.

She could not believe what she was seeing, yet a warmth was building in her, radiating out as she gazed on the smiling faces around her.

Max, Joe, Cami, and Lucy, arms linked, made their way out of the crowd and gestured to everyone to be quiet. Then they turned to Ms. Marwich. "You've given the Angel Tree to our town for twenty-five years," Cami said, her eyes shining.

Max stepped forward. "And made so many of our wishes come true."

Joe cleared his throat. "You helped all of us see what Christmas really is."

"So now it's our turn to bring Christmas to you!" Lucy exclaimed. And everyone cheered.

Ms. Marwich was struck speechless. For twenty-five years she had kept her secret hidden, yet somehow these four had discovered the truth. And she could not imagine how, not when she'd covered her tracks so carefully. Yet as she looked at their faces beaming with pride, she couldn't help but feel grateful. After twenty-five years she was ready to be discovered.

Pat Jordan, the Pine River mayor, came forward. She smiled warmly at Ms. Marwich.

"We are so grateful for the generosity of spirit you have shown to our town," the mayor said in her clear voice. "The Angel Tree has brought hope to the people of Pine River when they needed it the most. And joy to every one of us who has borne witness to the acts of kindness it generated. So now, as token of our gratitude, we have some things for you."

The crowd parted, opening up a small path and it was only then that Ms. Marwich saw the towering Christmas tree in the corner of her living room, lit up with lights, blanketed in colorful decorations, and crowned with a shining gold star. Presents were piled beneath it and next to it stood a small display that was covered with an ivory cloth.

Mayor Jordan stopped next to the display and pulled off the cloth with flourish. Underneath was a plaque and from where she was standing Ms. Marwich could make out the words *The Angel Tree* in elegant letters.

"First, a gift from our town," Mayor Jordan said. "This sign will be put in the town square, in front of the spot where the Angel Tree goes up each year. And if I can read it to you," she said turning to face the sign, then clearing her throat. " 'The Angel Tree, honoring Rona Berle Marwich, beloved member of the Pine River community.' "

Ms. Marwich teared up at the heartfelt simplicity of the words.

"The whole town is going to help you with the Angel Tree next year," the mayor added. "And now let me turn this over to the people gathered here." She smiled at Ms. Marwich. "There are an awful lot of folks here who want to give you something."

"And we're first," Cami said, pulling Lucy along with her, Max and Joe coming up behind.

Next to Joe stood a woman with large brown eyes just like Joe's, and the same shy sweet smile. "Ms. Marwich, I'd like you to meet my mom," Joe said, radiating happiness as his mom reached out to shake Ms. Marwich's hand.

"It's an honor to meet a soldier serving our country," Ms. Marwich said. "And I have to tell you we're all pretty fond of your boy around here."

Ms. Thompson ruffled Joe's hair affectionately. "Thank you for looking out for him," she said. "And for the wonderful gift you've been giving this town for so long. I think a lot of people are waiting to thank you for that."

"Starting with us," Cami said.

"The four of you figured this out, didn't you?" Ms.

Marwich asked, her eyes filling up again. Ed Pink passed her a handkerchief that she used to dab her eyes.

"Actually it was Lucy," Cami said proudly.

"It was all of us," Lucy said quickly. But Ms. Marwich detected a sparkle of pride in Lucy's face that had not been there before.

"And we got you something," Max said. He handed Ms. Marwich a gift.

Ms. Marwich pulled at the paper and then opened the thick square box inside. It contained a bound leather book but on top of that was the bookmark Ms. Marwich's grandmother had given her, a family heirloom she had treasured until last month when it had somehow gotten lost.

"I thought this was gone for good," Ms. Marwich said, picking it up in wonder. "Wherever did you find it?"

"Valentine sniffed it out at Pine Forest," Lucy said proudly.

"I'm thrilled to have it back," Ms. Marwich said. Then she grinned at the foursome. "Pine Forest, eh? You were really doing your homework. I didn't have a chance of keeping my secret, did I?"

The four of them laughed.

Ms. Marwich turned her attention to the leather book, pulling it out of the box and opening to the first page. It was a photo album entitled *The Angel Tree*. Ms. Marwich began to turn through the pages slowly. The book was filled with pictures of people together with their gifts from the Angel Tree. There was Olivia wearing a new dress and posing proudly by her new sewing machine. Lana Levkov and her mother were holding up a tray of the cream puffs her mother had been yearning for. And then there was one of the Callahan family and the crew assembled to build their new house, gathered around the building plan created by Lucy's father. Each shot was of something precious and each one filled Ms. Marwich with joy.

"I don't know what to say," the librarian said, finally looking up from the book she would cherish forever.

"Better get keep moving," Ed Pink said in his jovial way. "You've got a lot more to open."

Sure enough as she looked around Ms. Marwich saw that nearly everyone was holding a package wrapped in Christmas paper.

"And those there are from the folks who couldn't be here tonight," Mr. Pink added, gesturing to the pile under the tree.

Ms. Marwich's heart swelled with gratitude for the people in this room, in this town, who had filled her life with love for the past thirty years. "Thank you," she said. "Thanks to all of you and a very Merry Christmas!"

Acknowledgments

I am enormously grateful to David Levithan, good friend and phenomenal story teller. Huge thanks to Emily Seife, editor extraordinaire, whose wisdom and insight were invaluable on this project. I am privileged to be represented by the unstoppable Sara Crowe. Eliot Schrefer and Marie Rutkoski are the best readers out there and it is my great fortune to have them in my corner. I am lucky to get support (writing and otherwise) from the awesome Debbi Michiko Florence, Donna Freitas, Lisa Graff, Rebecca Stead, Deborah Heiligman, Martin Wilson, Bill Konigsberg, Carolyn MacCullough, Barry Lyga, Kathryne Alfred, Kira Bazile, Josh Phillips, Rose Liebman, and Keri Rehfisch. And because they are spectacular I must also thank Greg, Erlan, Ainyr, Khai, Avi, Nghia, my mom, and the one who this book is for, my sister, Sam.

About the Author

Daphne Benedis-Grab grew up in a small town in upstate New York where Christmas was always her favorite holiday. She is the author of *Alive and Well in Prague, New York*, a young adult novel. She has worked a variety of jobs, including building houses for Habitat for Humanity in Georgia, organizing an after-school tutoring program in San Francisco, and teaching ESL in China. She now lives in New York City with her husband, two kids, and a cat, and still looks forward to celebrating Christmas every year. Learn more at www.daphnebg.com.